THE DESERT OF THE REAL

VOLUME I

*An anthology of short stories from a world
not too dissimilar to our own*

Matthew Watson

Clink
Street

Published by Clink Street Publishing 2023

Copyright © 2023

First edition.

ISBNs:
978-1-915229-87-8 Paperback
978-1-915229-88-5 Ebook

Harrison, Dexter and Maxwell,
For the times when I am not there

TABLE OF CONTENTS

PRIDE LANDS ON ITS BACK   1

MAKE ONE MAN WEEP, ANOTHER WOMAN SING   4

EIGHT YEARS LATER   34

FOMO   36

GREEN EYES AND HAM   41

THE HOUND AND HARE,
CHARING CROSS   46

ABJECTNATION   69

IT'S NOT THE END OF THE WORLD   70

CHUCK IT ON THE SCAPEGOAT   84

THOSE HURT IN THE DOORWAY OF CHANGE
WILL BE THOSE WHO STOOD STILL   86

SIX PICK UP STICKS   100

HERETIC'S DESCENT   118

THE ANNALS OF AMAR PLAYLIST   192

PRIDE LANDS ON ITS BACK

'This is completely unacceptable, brother; our father would have **never** allowed something so heinous.'

The two stared at each other with contempt, their stony expressions reflecting the walls of dark rock around them. The younger brother spoke again hastily before he could be interrupted.

'It is nothing short of genocide! They will all die of starvation if left banished outside our lands, please, brother, you must reconsider.'

The older brother chose his words carefully.

'As King… tough decisions must be made for the good of our people, you know this.'

'Outrageous!' the younger retorted. 'Our people are not in any danger! This decision is fuelled purely from your prejudice and inability to manage the different cultures you rule over.'

Had he have seen the king's nostrils flare sharply; he may not have continued with his tirade.

'…It is your duty to protect **all** those who live on our land, not just those of a similar ilk to you and myself. Your charge as king is to find a solution to suit the needs of the entire population, not simply to just kill off those who are bothersome to you. Brother, heed my warning I beg of you, if you do not use your crown fairly and with honour then you risk putting a target on your bac...'

The younger brother fell to the floor suddenly as a sharp pain erupted across his face, when he looked up, he saw the king towering above him.

'DO YOU THINK I AM SCARED OF YOUR THREATS, BROTHER?' the king roared, as his brother tried to stagger back to his feet beneath him. 'THEY ARE AN ABOMINATION TO OUR SOCIETY AND DO NOT DESERVE TO LIVE AMONGST US!' he bellowed.

The king leaned into his brother slowly, his voice now much lower and embittered.

'Too long we have allowed ourselves to co-exist with these inferior, cretinous savages. It is only a matter of time before their numbers become too great to manage and they challenge me for the throne... and I will **not** let our family's dynasty fall just because you've decided to grow a conscience! But if you care for hyenas, for vermin, to that considerable extent, brother, enough to threaten your king... then you are welcome to go out there and join them in desolation.'

The younger brother began to squint as blood from the wound seeped into his eye, he tried to sit up only to have his arms pinned to the ground.

The king lowered his voice to a whispering growl.

'Now I think you need to demonstrate some... loyalty. Yes, definitely. Loyalty, before I lose my temper again and give your other eye a scar.'

A smirk appeared on the king's face.

'Say those four words that I love to hear you say, brother.'

The returned silence irritated the king and in a flash of frustration he dug his claws deep into his brother's hands.

'Say it.'

'Please... I beg of you...'

'SAY IT'

'Long live... long live the king.'

'Good.'

The king pounced off his brother, sending hypnotic ripples across his cinnamon mane. The royal counsel, a fluttering hornbill, cut through the tense atmosphere and arrived to whisper news of the savanna into the King's ear. With a scornful look back to his brother, the lion turned to exit the cave with the hornbill in tow, leaving his brother to tend to his eye wound alone.

The Annals of Amar
MAKE ONE MAN WEEP, ANOTHER WOMAN SING

Sarah Atete

What is love? asked Haddaway in his 1993 breakout hit. It was a question that resonated with Sarah significantly at this point in her life and, like with many well-timed songs, she was convinced it was fate that it had started playing on her radio. Why wasn't there an answer for what love is yet? We had convincing theories for the birth of the universe and how atoms work.

Why was love still mostly a mystery?

The lack of an immediate answer bothered Sarah. Maybe asking Baby not to hurt you was enough of an answer for now.

The nostalgic journey through the Bambi years of '90s Dance ended with the arrival of the lunchtime news report. It was announcing a breakthrough in the understanding of emotions. Erogen, a lab in Halifax, Nova Scotia, had recently discovered that human emotions were actually tangible and existed in a physical form which could now be accessed, analysed and understood to a much greater level than previously thought.

The radio presenters pondered the ramifications of this find.

'Does this mean we could finally understand and study dreams too?'

A presenter then made the predictable joke of saying she would not want to know her co-host's dreams, followed by them both chuckling sensibly.

'But what else could this mean, Lauren?' pressed the presenter. 'Could we soon bottle emotions and sell them? What about negative emotions like hate and jealousy, could these be weaponised at all?'

The news segment continued to less philosophical matters. It was revealed that the information around the discovery appeared to have been leaked unofficially to the media before Erogen could hold its press conference. Sarah's thoughts naturally drifted to Clark and she wondered if the security breach was causing him any grief at work.

Suddenly disgusted with herself, Sarah stormed over to the fridge in an effort to distract herself from this toxic train of thought. Some days she thought she was making a lot of progress in coming to terms with the breakdown of her marriage, and then on others... bah. With this lapse threatening to remind herself of her loneliness, she decided to make lunch while she was in the kitchen.

The story of Sarah and Clark was one of a relationship that approached the rapid rocky waters of life's hardships, as many do, but capsized before making it past the first wave.

It began, as few do, with a murder.

It was two years prior and, as an acting inspector, Sarah rarely got involved with investigations at a frontline level. The interviewing of witnesses was for constables, if not sergeants, almost exclusively. However, with resources in the force at an all-time low as well as the opportunity to unashamedly show her superiors that she could still 'muck in', Sarah dispatched herself to the scene of a murder at Iridium Industries, just off the science park in town. It was here that Sarah first met who she thought to be her soulmate, Clark Atete, the security guard on duty that evening.

The murder of James Harnett turned out to be quite a simple case at face value. Iridium Industries, regularly the scene of intense protests from animal rights activists, was a well-known area of disturbance to the police. On this occasion, things had gotten out of hand, an individual had sneaked into the compound and confronted one of the scientists, James Harnett, while he crossed the courtyard into another of Iridium's labs.

The Incident, captured on CCTV, showed the confrontation rapidly escalating into a brawl, unfortunately resulting in James Harnett losing his life as he hit his head on the concrete, moments before the security guard, Clark, could arrive to help.

Despite the self-imposed guilt and grief for not being there sooner, Clark was instrumental to the investigation and through his identification of who eventually turned out to be a disgruntled ex-employee rather than a protestor, Sarah was able to arrest Hasira Fansa that night. All in all, a very quick and successful resolution.

After the investigation was tied up, what started simply as providing follow up reassurance and support to a key witness, quickly developed into Sarah and Clark spending increasing amounts of time together outside of work hours. Sarah had never felt chemistry like it, it was electrifying, exciting and, despite it starting under unorthodox and arguably unethical circumstances, a relationship soon blossomed.

Clark proposed to Sarah on their one-year anniversary and within six months they got married in a small ceremony just outside of Birmingham. The two were intoxicated with affection for each other and their happiness was the envy of everyone they knew.

Unfortunately, this bliss was not meant to last. Hasira Fansa, the killer of James Harnett, had launched an appeal into his conviction which was gaining momentum as Sarah and Clark focused on their future together. The defence, who appeared much more ruthless than their predecessors, uncovered some critical errors with the investigation, primarily from the key witness account, Clark's.

Inconsistencies with his witness statement and the timings on the CCTV revealed that he had not reacted to the brawl as quickly as he had initially stated, resulting in a re-trial and the ultimate release of Hasira. Clark was unceremoniously fired from Iridium Industries the moment the news of the trial broke. As a result of their relationship being dragged into the light and the integrity of Clark's statement resting upon Sarah's shoulders, she too faced the wrath of her employers and was given no choice but to resign from the force with immediate effect.

Blame erupted through the marriage like fissures of an earthquake and the two lovebirds were thrown into financial and emotional disarray. Sarah tried everything to make the relationship work, couples counselling, therapy, but Clark's lack of engagement in these measures meant they fell flat. Not long after they had begun sleeping in separate beds, Clark unexpectedly announced he had got a new job as a security guard in Canada, where he was to relocate immediately. Shocked at the speed that it was all falling apart, Sarah begged him to stay, a move that shamed her to this day.

During the months that followed, Sarah disgraced herself with an extensive Facebook and social media stalking campaign to find Clark, but the only snippet of information she uncovered was on a company's website, called Erogen labs, that listed him as their new head of security. She gave up the pursuit.

And with that, it all comes full circle. Seven months after Clark abandoned her, Sarah now stood in the kitchen with a large glass of wine for her lunch. As her mind continued to drift around the topic of love and its many mysteries and horrors, the sound of her doorbell brought her harshly back to reality. Irritated, she took a large swig of wine and went to answer the door. As she walked past the radio, a sentence caused her to linger:

'...*Erogen are expected to make a press conference this evening in which they will undoubtedly attempt to manage people's expectations, in their own words, on the announcement. The leak has caused colossal waves in the stock market and experts warn this may be premature depending on the realities of Erogen's findings. The company's inflated share price, which hasn't been this high since they split from Iridium Industries back in 2009, could leave investors red faced if...*'

'Hmm,' mused Sarah. That's interesting.

Hasira Fansa

The ivory keys felt cold beneath Hasira's fingers. He had not sat down to play piano for years now and the memory of exactly how to do it was escaping him. An unknown chord shape naturally took form on his fingers and as he pressed down, he realised that he was remembering the introduction to David Gray's 1998 hit, 'This Year's Love', an old favourite.

The muscle memory faded after the first few bars, however, leaving Hasira to sit there in silence with his thoughts. The respite turned out to be a fleeting one, as a sharp disturbance erupted from the wall behind him.

It had become increasingly obvious to Hasira that whoever introduced his neighbour to the band Joy Division did so without the forethought to say that they could continue to listen to other bands at the same time, it wasn't an exclusive relationship or at least shouldn't have been. The beginning of their compilation album *Substance* was vibrating through Hasira's wall for the third time this week and if he had to endure anymore of this sadistic, musical monogamy...

His train of thought, as well as Ian Curtis's tortured lyrics, thankfully, was quickly lost to the breaking story on the television to his side. Standing up as if to help him focus through the noise, Hasira let the details of Erogen's scientific achievement wash over him.

This was his cue.

Turning into the bedroom, Hasira dived hastily into the back of his cupboard to retrieve a small black duffle bag. He opened it to check its contents, the light chink of small clear vials of liquid satisfying his search before closing the bag again and turning to leave the apartment.

As he stepped away, the melody of 'Love Will Tear Us Apart' purred through the plasterboard around him.

This song in particular irked Hasira greatly. Impulsively he turned back to the room and went over to the HiFi on the wall, spinning the volume dial up aggressively and pressing play to whatever CD was currently inside. Without waiting to hear what track was hopefully going to ruin his neighbour's enjoyment of *Substance* next door, Hasira turned and left.

The walk did not take long, he had practiced this drill a few times since his release from prison. Reaching his destination, he placed the duffle bag on the ground to free up both hands, looking around for who was around the area. The lunchtime foot traffic meant this was going to have to be a quick and quiet affair, something he had not really planned for.

Hasira pressed the doorbell in front of him and waited.

The sound of a chain being unhooked the other side could be heard, and as he waited, Hasira wondered if Sarah would remember him.

Sarah Atete

Were this a Hollywood film, the subsequent scene would probably have been an adrenaline filled thrash of flying fists. Sharp orchestral noises would underlie the mounting tension as the two grappled for physical dominance. There would be flying furniture, a race to a knife block and someone being thrown through a window only for the fight to continue on the street outside.

In reality, the reactions of a woman who was drinking wine for lunch left much to be desired and Hasira managed to step inside and incapacitate Sarah with ease before she even had time to let go of the door chain.

Sarah awoke to a groggy sensation some minutes later, bound tightly to one of her own chairs. Her head was throbbing from where the intruder had hit her and as her vision slowly returned, she began to recognise the man kneeling on the ground before her.

'…Think..think about what you are doing…' she muttered in a low groan.

It was not unheard of for criminals to seek out the officers that incarcerated them. Most, however, tempered their desires before they acted in fear of their newly found freedom being removed once more.

Clearly, Hasira Fansa needed reminding of this and so Sarah continued to appeal to his reason.

'I'm sure… I'm sure you know that I am no longer in the force, Hasira, but any action against me will be treated the same as if I was. This isn't worth it.'

If Hasira was paying attention, he did not act like it. His hands were buried into his duffle bag along with his concentration. Sarah took the opportunity to fill the silence with some suggestions on what he could do instead of harming her. Her list started with sensible ideas such as visiting support groups or just moving away to start a new life. As his silence continued, however, this ultimately turned to offering electricals and other various possessions around her as bribes. The increasingly panicked suggestions soon tailed off as Sarah saw Hasira remove a syringe and vial of clear liquid from his bag.

Fight or flight set in. Sarah tried to kick and struggle but the binds on her wrists and ankles were far too strong, this was neither fighting nor flying, she thought, frustrated, just an adrenaline rush stuck to a chair like some sort of nightmare roller coaster.

'Hasira PLEASE!'

To her dismay the plea appeared to fall upon deaf ears. Hasira nonchalantly stepped towards her, pinning her right arm down onto the chair arm. With his free hand he slid back her sleeve past the elbow, casually plunging the syringe into her arm.

Sarah was not sure if it was whatever was in Hasira's syringe or her fear that made her pass out again, but this time, before she slipped into the black, her mind unsurprisingly went back to Clark.

Clark Atete

'It concerns me greatly, Mr Atete, that you have no idea how this leak occurred.'

Dr Amar was sitting behind an unnecessarily grand desk, his chair reclining slightly as he took a pause in the conversation to slowly clean his glasses. They were not dirty, but Clark suspected that it was all part of the uncomfortable suspense Amar wanted to build.

He ignored the performance.

'As I said, sir, we found no records of intrusion on our systems, it must have been an internal release. I have my men now interviewing the staff to ascertain...'

'Mmm,' Amar cut in, causing Clark to pause. 'But who watches the watchmen, Mr Atete?'

'I'm sorry, sir, I don't follow?'

Dr Amar finished cleaning his glasses and slowly stood up from his seat. He made sure to make his steps sound timed and deliberate as he walked around the desk to lean his back against it, now much closer to Clark. He appeared to choose his next words carefully.

'What you did for me, for this company and for our vision... back at Iridium Industries, was nothing short of inspired. Your job, its salary and the relocation here to Nova Scotia is hopefully more than enough of a thank you for what was quite a large undertaking on your part.'

Amar did not give Clark time to respond to this.

'What Iridium Industries taught me, or more to the point, what Dr Harnett's betrayal taught me, is that... trust leaves you vulnerable, trust leaves you open. Now, because of the nature of our work, I can't afford to be caught with my trousers down like I was then, not when we are **this** close.'

He squinted, pincering his thumb and index finger together for effect. Clark carefully nodded, he felt himself beginning to sweat and it wasn't something he wanted Amar to notice.

'In what could probably be described as an over-cautious or even paranoid move, when we moved operations to Halifax I employed the resources of a 'shadow' security service, essentially a second ring of defence, that would monitor our company from afar, off the books, and in the background.' Amar watched Clark's expression carefully as he spoke.

'…And to cut a long story short, Mr Atete, as we are both busy people… it appears from the evidence presented to me this morning by this team, that it was in fact… yourself? who leaked the information to the pre…'

The atmosphere in the room was pierced by the psyche-delic introduction to Chris Isaac's 'Wicked Game' radiating from the phone in Clark's pocket and abruptly cutting Amar off. Clark nudged the volume button through his trouser pocket to mute the call, relishing the annoyance that flashed across Amar's face at his dramatic moment being soured.

Before his hand moved away from his pocket, he felt a small vibration of a further message being received. It will have to be a message left unread, thought Clark, knowing exactly who the not-so-mystery caller was by the contact assigned ringtone.

The missed call alone was enough for Clark to know he could face his imminent curtain call without fear, or too much of it at least.

Hasira Fansa

Hasira placed his phone down and walked over to the unconscious woman in front of him. Could he have been a little less forceful?

Perhaps, he admitted. Would Sarah have injected herself eventually had he have explained the situation? Most likely. But Hasira didn't have the time nor the patience these days, those were luxuries he lost long ago.

Removing a small chalk of ammonia from his pocket, he hovered it just under Sarah's nose and broke it in half. With a jolt, Sarah was back in the land of the living.

'Wha… whaaah?… AHHHHHH!!!'

Hasira quickly placed a hand over her mouth to subdue the shrill screams. He met her wide-eyed state and spoke softly.

'Ms Atete, listen to me. To say that we are short of time would be a gross understatement. I will explain everything to you as quickly as I can, however, to start off I need you to stop screaming, are you going to comply? I can assure you that you are in no danger from myself.'

Time was not actually too much of an issue for the two of them right now if he was being honest, but Hasira wanted to drum up a bit of urgency to get things moving and hopefully prevent too many unnecessary questions.

Almost as if in defiance to this deceit, he suddenly felt Sarah's teeth sinking into his palm and had to hold back a howl of his own. His voice now became less soft.

'Sarah, I can understand the animosity believe me but realise that if this were an attempt on your life in any way then I wouldn't have woken you up, nor would I have rung the bloody doorbell!' He began to untie Sarah from the chair, seemingly unconcerned about any danger she could pose to him once free. He did however sense an attempt to escape was on the horizon, so he chose to disarm her with a question.

'Can you tell me how you feel about Clark Atete right at this moment?'

Clark Atete

Dr Amar smiled to himself and walked back around his desk, talking as he went.

'I must say I was surprised you came into the office today, Clark, either you were too stupid to realise you would get caught or thought yourself brave enough to face the repercussions of your actions.'

As he spoke, Amar pulled open a drawer and took out a cloudy vial of liquid, placing it carefully on the table.

'...So, which is it, stupidity or bravery?'

Clark's attention dropped briefly to the vial between them. He raised his gaze to meet Amar's once more, continuing his silence. Dr Amar carried on his monologue pretending the question was rhetorical, the small flicker of his teeth clenching gave away his irritation at being ignored however.

'You, more than most, Mr Atete, should know how important confidentiality is in our line of work. If the public found out what we were capable of before we were ready... then it would all be for nothing.' Dr Amar paused for effect before continuing.

'By throwing our research into the spotlight in such a way you have put me in a very... uncomfortable position. I am simply not ready for the world to know the extent of what we can achieve, and I clearly can't keep someone under my employ who would openly betray our vision. It is clear you didn't learn anything from the death of James Harnett, did you, Mr Atete?'

Clark raised his eyebrows slightly to Amar's question but again spoke no words. These were likely to be his last living moments and he was not going to give Amar the satisfaction of looking scared.

'...in contrast, however, I did learn something from James' death,' continued Amar. 'Killing someone off is a messy and problematic affair which meant, as you well know, a considerable amount of effort must be spent after the fact moving pieces around the chessboard to get back to normality. Instead, there are... cleaner options.' And with this he pushed the vial towards Clark.

Clark slowly drew in a deep breath and sighed loudly, he had been banking on a quick and easy death, but he should have known Amar would want to play with his food.

'I am not afraid to die, Amar,' he said while meeting Amar's gaze. 'But if you think I'm going to willingly take one of your serums then you are not nearly as intelligent as you want everyone to think.'

'How gallant and bullish of you.' Amar smiled thinly, unsurprised at Clark's retort. 'However, you will be quite frustrated, I imagine, to hear that you have already been exposed to this serum. I laced the chair you are sitting in with it before you came in.'

Sarah Atete

The question hit her like a freight train, but not for the reasons she was anticipating. She expected her blood to boil upon hearing Hasira even mentioning Clark's name after all the pain and suffering he had caused them and their relationship. She imagined she would say something dramatic to him like, '... You don't ever get to mention his name in my presence...' and perhaps point threateningly, but instead there was... nothing.

No feelings at all for Clark Atete.

Sarah suddenly felt very off-balance and exposed. It was as if her ears had just popped after a long flight. The weight of the heartbreak she had been carrying the past few months had evaporated at the mention of his name, leaving only confusion as to why she had cared so much in the first place.

Her expression or lack of response must have exposed her, because Hasira was now nodding reassuringly and offered his hand to help her from the chair. She did not take it.

Unfazed, Hasira retracted it, breaking the silence.

'You have unfortunately been used as a pawn in a game you didn't even know you were a part of, Sarah.'

'That is actually a bit too **fucking** vague, Hasira,' Sarah snapped. 'Do you mind telling me why you are here? What you injected me with and wh...'

'STOP,' barked Hasira, his eyes wide and a flat hand held up in Sarah's direction. 'I was getting to that.' He lowered the hand but kept his gaze stern, daring Sarah to challenge him.

'The CEO of Iridium Industries and Erogen, Dr Amar, has for some time been in possession of a means to control people, more specifically, their ability to love. The news reports you have undoubtedly seen today only scratch the surface at what Amar is capable of doing and has been actively doing in secret. The specifics of how this works are complex and you do not need to know them, but essentially it is to do with a serum he can administer which is engineered to make the recipient feel strong feelings of love or lust for whoever or whatever he chooses. As you can imagine, this gives the doctor an unimaginable amount of power to do just about anything he wants. The possibilities are sickening. He can make people love him, his ideas, his rule! He could force adversaries to fall for destructive tendencies or manipulate a population to love their land enough to go to war for it. Essentially, Dr Amar's discovery has given him the ability to play God with the hearts of all of us.'

Noticing Sarah's increased agitation, Hasira brought the scope of the conversation back to her.

'Onto how this impacts you personally. You will remember the name Dr James Harnett I have no doubt. James was the only man who saw this threat coming and tried to stop Amar before he was in an untouchable position. Back at Iridium Industries, James developed in secret a formula that he hoped would negate the effects of Amar's serum. Unfortunately, however, Amar discovered James' efforts and had him... removed.'

Hasira paused, presumably to ensure Sarah was keeping up. Hasira's tale sounded fanatical and completely absurd, yet something was preventing her from dismissing it entirely. Perhaps it was the old detective brain whirling once more, but she needed to hear all the details and so nodded to Hasira to continue.

'The killing of James Harnett was one of many with Amar's fingerprints on it, but his personal attachment to the situation and haste to control it made for quite a clumsy execution, requiring an elaborate cover up operation for him after the fact. Clark and I were the night shift security at Iridium that night and were instrumental to Amar's alibi. I was forced to kill and take the blame for James' death, with the condition I would be released upon the later collapse of the trial. To ensure this, Amar worked his magic to make sure that the attending police officer was to fall head over heels in love with the main witness...'

It was becoming harder to tell herself that Hasira was lying now. Something about the picture that he was painting she knew to be true. To be used in such a grotesque, immaterial and dispensable way made Sarah feel physically sick and disgusted. Her thoughts flitted back to various victims of sexual assaults that she had dealt with as a police officer. Is this what it felt like? A powerless sensation overwhelmed her.

'This ultimately brings me onto why I am here now, Sarah, and this is important.' Hasira crouched down to where Sarah was cradling her head with her hands. 'Clark and I have been working together to pick up where James left off. Since moving to Halifax and under the guise of being indebted to Amar for his new life, Clark has been working to destroy the research and serum housed at Erogen Labs. You see we could not move against Amar without ensuring that his work couldn't be continued by the next deranged lunatic who will step in to fill Amar's void. Once all was in place, Clark was to land a killing blow to Amar's secret campaign by releasing confidential Erogen information to the press, shining the light on Amar and his activities. This media release was also a signal to me to find you and release you of Amar's affliction with one of James' antidotes, a stipulation to the plan that Clark was very adamant about.'

This was a lot to take in all at once, thought Sarah. Where do you even begin with something like this? Releasing her head from her hands she stood up slowly and looked around the room for inspiration of somewhere to start. Her eyes landed on the open bag of vials at Hasira's feet.

'Why do you have so many vials? Do the effects of James' antidote wear off? Or are there others you intend to inject with strange liquids?'

Her head was spinning.

'This is all James was able to make before Amar caught him,' replied Hasira as he lightly nudged the duffle bag with his foot. 'This final version hadn't been tested prior to his death so I have no way of knowing if its effects are temporary or not. James told me that he managed to fix the flaws in the last batch however so I'm hopeful that...'

'Flaws? What flaws?' interrupted Sarah, nostrils flared. 'So, what, you are just using me as a guinea pig to see if this stuff even works? What sort of backwards, cowboy, mad-scientist...'

'We know it works,' muttered Hasira softly. 'Because we had to use it on me.'

James Harnett
The night before his death

James could not sleep again. The oscillating fan next him normally provided soothing white noise but tonight his mind was too wired to drift off. He sat up to turn it off and let out a small sigh.

A broken voice came from the pillows next to him.

'You've been fidgeting all night... What's going on?'

James had half hoped his restlessness would cause Hasira to stir, he needed to talk things through with him.

'Has... I think it's time.'

Hasira sat up hastily and placed a gentle hand on the back of James' neck.

'No, nono don't say that, things were just starting to settle back down again, maybe we don't have to do this, maybe there are options we haven't thought of?' Hasira spoke quickly, it was clear he had been prepared for this conversation.

James moved a hand to the back of his neck as well, placing it reassuringly on top of Hasira's. He looked out of the window in thought. 'Unfortunately, not. Amar and I finally clashed yesterday at the board meeting. I accused him of betraying the core values of the company and he accused me of trying to sabotage him, it's clear from the meeting that he knows about the antidote.'

He didn't need to go into details, Hasira knew of the conflict that had been brewing between the two old friends for some time.

Amar and James had met at university many years before Hasira came on the scene. James described his friendship with Amar at that time as one born from the universal rejection from the rest of their peers, they were outcasts. As time went on the two depended on each other more and more, their affinity for science bonding them and their grand plans on saving the world led to dreams of wacky inventions and science fiction solutions.

From this, the idea of Iridium Industries was born. The two scientists found early success with various small-scale products which ultimately bankrolled the larger company mission: to investigate and understand human emotions.

Perhaps instigated by the rejection of those around them or because neither of them had ever had a relationship, the ability to understand and manipulate desire and lust in particular became the main focus point for James and Amar.

The first seed of conflict between the two friends came from Amar's insistence that all research into this area must be hidden and kept off the books until they were in a position for their work to make a real change in society. James had disagreed at the time, concerned about Amar's motives and wanting their work to be available to all, but he ultimately relented.

Iridium Industries was then split, with the original company operating publicly and generating profit through various unrelated scientific services and a second company, Erogen, created to work solely on James and Amar's mission to understand and control love in the background.

It was around this time that Hasira came on the scene. Employed as the night shift security for Iridium Industries, Hasira soon became friendly with the only other person he saw during his patrol of the grounds each night, an overworked and mentally over encumbered James Harnett.

In Hasira, James found something which had been missing his entire life. The anger and bitterness that had propelled his and Amar's work seemed to chip away from James the more time the two spent together, and before long he found himself, not only in his first ever relationship but, for once, happy.

Was it jealousy that Amar felt as he watched his friend achieve a happiness he felt he could never obtain himself? Or was it abandonment, that it was no longer the two of them against the institution of relationships and of love? Whatever Amar felt internally, his personality grew colder and crueller to those around him.

'He is right though Has. I have changed. I have not agreed with our work for some time. And now that Amar thinks he's cracked it…'

'What!? I thought his serum was denied to progress to human trials?' retorted Hasira, alarmed. James sighed.

'It appears that it doesn't matter anymore, Amar has been getting what he wants more and more these days, often against logic… I fear that we are past the point where trials are necessary…'

Hasira sat up now too. They knew this day would one day loom, but it was one Hasira had hoped they would not have to face for some time. The two had suspected that Amar's research into love had uncovered a way for him to control it for a while now. With James no longer there to neutralise Amar's more extreme ambitions, it was inevitable that he would use his discovery for nefarious means. Critics had rescinded on their words and become devotees, former competitors had become keen collaborators, inexplicably offering up their resources to help further Amar's work. James had casually questioned him on these unusual occurrences at the time, but Amar just smiled and shrugged them away.

Bodies had begun to fall around him too. People who had maybe gotten too close to the truth of his work or had irked Amar in some way appeared to find themselves at a grisly end one way or another. To their knowledge, Amar had never got his hands dirty himself, but it was noticed that those ultimately arrested for the killings would often be found to have, at best, an intense fascination with Amar, and at worst, a deep and all-consuming infatuation.

It was because of this that James and Hasira knew that soon the time would come when they too would have a target painted on their backs. With so few aware of Amar's corrupted and sinister intentions, coupled with this now limitless power and control over a person's emotions, running away from the problem was just not an option. James and Hasira felt they needed to stay and dismantle Amar's work from the inside, otherwise who else was left to stop him?

There was no doubt to them both that, should the time come when Amar needed one of them gone, he would relish the opportunity to exert his own twisted poetic justice and have the other land the killing blow. Their only option now, was a small vial of liquid that James now held in his hand. The two men stared at it for some time before talking long into the night, both going back and forth on what to do.

After some time, Hasira's alarm for work broke the atmosphere in the room. James crouched down in front of him and took his hands.

'Has... many don't get to choose how they die or who they die with. I am in the rare position of being able to choose both. I want the last thing I see on this world to be your face. I want to fall into whatever darkness awaits me knowing that I am in the arms of the man I love and that in my last moments on this earth... he will be holding me.' He squeezed Hasira's hands tightly as tears fell to them. James continued.

'Once Amar has made his move and believes you to be in love with him and under his control, you must do what he says... for this is the only way we can continue to fight against him, under the radar. If this formula works, your ability to feel emotions will be gone, protecting you from

Amar's influence. It will mean, unfortunately, that you won't love me anymore when it happens... but hopefully something inside you will remember us this...' They shared a kiss that seemed to last a lifetime. Eventually Hasira broke it off, softly.

'I don't know if I want to live in a world where I don't love you, James.'

'But you must, Has, you must! Never give up, or we will have lost, all of us, to whatever dystopian world Amar wants to create for mankind.' Hasira did not respond, he knew James was right, but it was a reality he was struggling to come to terms with.

'Alexa, play Meatloaf, "I Would Do Anything For Love",' announced Hasira coolly to the room, James looked at him bemused. '...This... this would have been our wedding song had we have...you know, gotten there.' They shared a tragic laugh, there was so much left to say. Hasira held out his hand. 'Dance with me?'

The two lovers shared their last dance. A message came through to Amar's phone at some point during the last chorus; *Please can you report to my office asap before starting work, thanks, Amar.*

Hasira Fansa

'The initial formula was more of a preventative measure than an actual cure to Amar's serum,' he added to Sarah after finishing off the small history of James, Amar, and himself. 'It was put together when the likelihood of Amar using his serum on me to murder James became likely.' Hasira used the break in conversation to check the window for anyone who may have heard the earlier scuffle between him and Sarah. There was no one outside.

'But why didn't you both just run away or tell the police?' Sarah implored. 'I can't understand why James had to die at all?'

'Once Amar had made the decision to have James killed, he was on borrowed time. You are a living example of Amar's power over the Criminal Justice System so going to the police would have been ultimately fruitless. We were potentially the last two people on earth who could do something to stop Amar from using his serum. James came up with the idea that if I were to feign loyalty to Amar, pretend to be under 'spell' so to speak, his guard would be lowered, and I might one day find a window of opportunity to stop all this from growing out of control. I can assure you that we explored every possible option, but the only answer ultimately was for James to sacrifice himself.'

Sarah chose her next words carefully.

'You sound quite... nonchalant about the death of your partner.'

Hasira did not turn to face her.

'As I said, the antidote I took the night of James' death was a preventative measure and it worked. Amar's serum had no impact on me when the time came... because I could no longer feel emotions anyway. Fortunately, this made killing James a whole lot easier than it would have been otherwise, I believe, but the 'flaw' I alluded to earlier was that it has prevented me from feeling anything since.'

Sarah said nothing. *Of course,* she accepted with disbelief. *Of course, the man standing in my house is now an actual psychopath. That is just what was missing from this situation. Brilliant.*

Sarah thought back to the Judge's comments at Hasira's trial, lamenting him for appearing 'remorseless' and 'callous' in the face of the killing. He had stood in that courtroom with the same piercing emptiness that he showed her now. As she scanned his face for a trace of emotion, Hasira bent down to brandish a beige piece of paper from his bag and held it out to her.

'This is for you, from Clark.'

She reached out with trepidation, the knowledge of Hasira's emotional state gave Sarah the impression he was suddenly unpredictable and, although she convinced herself that this was the reason for her cautious reach, the reality was she was nervous about what this letter might say.

Hasira shook the paper impatiently before dropping it into Sarah's lap and turning back to look out the window. Hesitantly, Sarah looked down and unfolded the letter.

To Sarah,

Sorry simply isn't enough. Nor is my apology something you should ever accept. The fact you are reading this letter means Hasira has reached you and rid you of your affliction. I pray now that after all this is over you may now go on to have a normal life and find someone you truly love. You deserve nothing less. Though this news undoubtedly casts a very dark cloud over your memories of our relationship, I look back on our time together with great fondness and wish I could have known you under different circumstances.

Through the chaos and hurt I hope you can understand what Hasira and I are trying to achieve. Dr Amar is simply far too dangerous to leave unchallenged and it would make a mockery of James' sacrifice if we didn't throw everything we could into unseating him. Hopefully at the time of reading I have been able to lift the veil of secrecy at Erogen. Soon, governments around the world should all be aware of the technology discovered there and greater minds than ours can think of how to contain this danger going forward – a treaty similar to nuclear weapons perhaps? Who knows.

Maybe down the line this can be used for good. The

phrase 'Find a job you love, and you'll never have to work another day in your life' springs to mind. Maybe as a society we could be happier if we loved the right things – Children struggling at school could be given a love for learning, we as a society could be given a love for protecting the environment, for each other... endless uses. Dreams for another lifetime, I guess.

The last stage of the plan is for you and Hasira to face. Listen to him, he has got more motive than anyone to get this done right and hopefully it's an incentive you both now share. We have worked together in the shadows for years now and I trust with his expertise you will both finish this.

Has – I will be up there with James cheering you on, good luck

– Clark.

Sarah read the letter through again to fully absorb what she was reading. An hour ago, reading a letter from Clark would have set her heart racing, now... well her heart was still racing but for different reasons, most likely the lunatic standing in front of her window with a bag of syringes at his feet.

A thousand questions were still swirling inside her head and she was struggling to find a place to start making sense of all this. She decided to start with the latest mystery.

'What does he mean by 'I'll be up there with James?''

Hasira did not turn away from the window as he spoke.

'The last stage of the plan is for us to attend Clark's funeral.'

Clark Atete

His trip back to the security office was a slow one. It meandered around the grounds of Erogen Labs in what he justified to himself as 'the scenic route', albeit one of concrete and wire fences.

The meeting with Amar had ended abruptly after the whole serum-on-the-chair reveal. He had told Clark that he had another meeting to attend to and ushered him to return to the office to clear out his desk. It was strange, thought Clark, that given the context of their meeting Amar was keen for Clark to walk freely from the compound. He could not focus on that just yet really as there were more pressing matters.

The plan was still mostly on track, Clark and Hasira had accommodated for a few deviations. Plan A revolved around the strong possibility that Amar was just going to kill Clark there and then once he found out about the leak. This would have forced Amar to arrange another elaborate excuse for Clark's death, similar to James', almost certainly resulting in him attending Clark's funeral, where Hasira and hopefully Sarah, would also be in attendance ready to kill him.

It was the only opportunity that all three individuals would be in the same space without raising Amar's suspicions; Sarah as the heartbroken ex looking to say one final goodbye, and Hasira as Clark's old world colleague, potentially exploiting the occasion of a funeral to see Amar again due his supposed infatuation with him. To everyone else, Hasira would be there as the accused criminal, glad to see the man who testified against him lowered into the ground. It should not look out of place for them both to be there – it was flawless.

It was also potentially one of the few places where Amar would be vulnerable. Hasira and Clark had known about his 'Shadow Security Service' for some time and their 24/7 protection around Amar had scuppered many a plan to get to him. Even at Erogen, there was a strict no weapons policy with all employees being searched before entering. The funeral would be the only exposure Amar would have to an uncontrolled environment in some time.

With Clark walking out of the office alive, however, they needed to switch to plan B. He was to go home and take a lethal overdose of morphine, leaving behind a suicide note that would very subtly suggest that he collaborated with another person at Erogen to leak the information. This would hopefully lure Amar to the funeral anyway, keen to look out for potential collaborators who may be amongst the grieving.

In all honesty, Clark did not mind that they were forced to use plan B. The morphine option was undoubtedly a much more peaceful end compared to whatever Amar might have been capable of in his office. Even the issue of Amar's dramatic mic-drop, the chair-serum, was not too much of a concern.

They had anticipated that Amar may do to Clark what he believed he did to Hasira back at Iridium. Clark was not allowed to know the exact details of what they would do in this situation (in case he blurted it all out to Amar as part of a love-induced confession) but Hasira was confident he knew what to do in this situation, and Clark was content with that.

As Clark walked around assuring himself all was in hand, something was bothering him. Despite being supposedly infected, he did not feel any feelings of attractions or lust towards Amar.

That's fine, thought Clark in an attempt to put it out of his mind, *because it doesn't matter what effect the serum has on me, I'm just going to go home and get the job done.* Putting it out of his mind, Clark finished his walk with one last look back at Erogen Labs.

'We got you, you piece of shit,' he muttered under his breath, opening the door to his office.

Immediately he knew something was wrong, someone had been in the office. A small note lay squarely on top of his keyboard.

Feel free to use this...

Clark moved his mouse cautiously and scanned the screen. A small but precise suicide note was on the forefront of the screen, written impersonally and extremely generic.

What was more concerning was that this note was tactfully placed over what can only be described as a collection of the worst type of pornography imaginable. Suddenly the extent of Amar's depravity was made clear and his intention for the chair-serum no longer a mystery.

Looks like it's an ad-hoc plan C then decided Clark, brashly backspacing the suicide note on his screen and closing down the heinous images behind, albeit with an impulsive sense of reluctance that ashamed him greatly.

Returning to his home was now out of the question, it was clear he was going to be a danger to the public if he left this office, anything could happen if he were left with these destructive, manifesting thoughts. He thought of the school near his home. This had to be done here, and quickly.

'Sick bastard,' muttered Clark again, casually removing his belt and looking for a supportive beam above that could take his weight. Through his disgust at the levels Dr Amar was willing to go to quietly kill him off, Clark took solace in the fact that Amar was playing into their hands nicely anyway. *This is essentially actually still plan A*, he mused, placing a chair under the beam. *Plan A with extra steps.*

With a suitable beam located, Clark prepared for the end. At the outset of this plan Clark was slightly worried the fear of death would prevent him from doing what needed to be done, however the ever-increasing desire to focus on what he had seen on his screen kept him focused luckily, but he still needed to be quick.

Clark withdrew his phone to see Hasira's missed call and follow up message that was simply a link to the Fleetwood Mac song 'Silver Springs'. Clark cracked a brief smile at Hasira's choice to inform him that Sarah had been reached. He wondered if Hasira's sense of humour was potentially still there under all the brooding.

Clark let Stevie Nicks' vocals serenade him one last time as he finished the last of the preparation, wishing her otherwise silken vocals were coming out of something other than his tinny phone speakers.

Once finished, Clark looked to send his last message back, the vital last step to inform Hasira that the deed was about to be done. He lingered momentarily over Joy Division's 'Love Will Tear Us Apart' and the thought of Hasira's disgust at receiving this song again returned another small smile.

Too on the nose though, all things considered... thought Clark, looking at the belt in his hand and instead selected a song that he hoped would reach Hasira where nothing had in a long time.

Great Tune!! I've been listening to a bit of this recently.

The message was short and kept the illusion of a casual conversation. Below it Clark shared a link to Coldplay's 'The Scientist', threw his phone to the side and stood up on the chair in front of him.

Sarah Atete

The faint sound of a phone vibrating could be heard from the other side of the room. Sarah watched as Hasira reached into his pocket and nodded softly to his screen. They had not spoken in almost 20 minutes now, Sarah still had questions but took the break in the conversation to reflect on everything she had learned so far.

Hasira, on the other hand, was busy packing up his stuff and helping himself to items in Sarah's fridge, seemingly content with how everything had gone.

'We will need to travel separately to maintain the illusion that we are journeying to Clark's funeral independently.' Hasira munched, apple in hand. 'News should break of his death within 24 hours, I will leave tomorrow. You should wait a couple of days, as if toying with the idea of if you should go or not, then leave.'

Sarah did not respond, she looked out of the window for inspiration.

'Sarah if you don't think you can do this then you need to tell me now,' Hasira pressed.

She snapped her head towards him.

'I'm just trying to figure out a way that this can be handled without more bloodshed, Hasira, it's barbaric, all of it!' She took the opportunity of the outburst to question him again without the risk of receiving another insulting raised palm. 'I don't know why you even need me anyway, surely just you alone could kill this doctor?'

Hasira crunched into the apple again, clearly buying time to answer.

'I need you there to watch everyone *but* me and Dr Amar. When I have done what needs to be done… the reactions of the others at the scene should let us know if they are under any illusions of love for Amar. These people are who we need to target with the rest of James' antidote and hopefully turn into allies, the more people we convert to our cause early on the quicker we can eradicate the threat and destroy Amar's research.' He hesitated before continuing. '…But I understand if you feel like what I am asking is too much of an undertaking, it's not fair of me or Clark to assume you will be up for this.'

There was that name again, Clark. After the madness that was this afternoon, Sarah did not know what that name meant to her anymore.

No longer did it illicit the feelings of heartbreak and longing she had grown familiar with over the last two years, but nor did it fill her with the white-hot anger and disgust it had earlier upon hearing that their marriage and love was a lie. Instead, Clark's name now left Sarah with a confused feeling. One of sorrow, a reflection of the miserable end he had to face all alone, but also one of what could only be described as 'responsibility'. Artificial or not, her and Clark were a large part of each other's lives and with his passing it was down to someone to pick up the baton and carry on.

'I'll do it,' announced Sarah, standing with resolution. Hasira nodded softly in acceptance.

'I'll see you in Canada in about a week,' he concluded, throwing the apple core in the bin, shouldering the black duffle bag, and leaving without another word.

EIGHT YEARS LATER

A dishevelled radio lay among the rubble of a makeshift shelter, crackling and transmitting to the empty woods around it. Its owner had left in a hurry, knocking it to the ground where it would play until the fading batteries slowly silenced it.

'...that track was from Huey Lewis and the News, folks, made for the classic 1985 film *Back to the Future*. Before we move to the next track, Lauren, I believe you have some breaking news for us?'

'Thanks, Aaron, yes, fresh off the back of the renewed interest earlier in the week we've just received a report from the AIJ that the wanted terrorist Sarah Atete has been captured alive and is now in custody. A trial is being arranged in the coming weeks, but sources close to the AIJ are saying that she may just be given a death sentence as early as Friday.'

'Wow that's huge! Thank the Leader, I'm sure many of our listeners will feel safe and secure knowing that the Institute of Justice has done what they set out to do and squashed insurgency in our streets. With Atete captured surely that ends the threat of anti-Amarism?'

'I should hope so, Aaron, that's it from me, back at midday.'

'Thanks, Lauren, a fantastic result. Coming up next we

have one of the latest releases from the Amar Institute of Music which I know you guys are going to absolutely **love**, but first to conclude our retro throwback to a time before the AIM dominated the charts, here's grunge rockers Pearl Jam with 'Black', enjoy.'

FOMO

Zara grimaced slightly at the depressing state of her surroundings. The cocktail of body odours and cheap beer was something she did not have too much exposure to before and did not plan on revisiting in a hurry. This Massachusetts existed as a very different entity to where she had come from, and just seeing people out and mingling without their Compliance Drones felt alien and unnerving to her.

They do not know how good they have it.

Zara was not here to critique the nightlife of 2002, nor was she here to cater to the advances of the lonely men that kept approaching her. Her eyes stayed fixed on the door, waiting for her mark to enter the bar.

She smiled thinly at her own joke, the man she was waiting for was actually called Mark and just as the latest peacocking male gave up attempting to talk to her, Zara saw him walk in with a close-knit gaggle of his peers. He looked different in the flesh, shyer and innocent with more than an air of insecurity maybe. Zara studied him from afar for a moment and watched as he nervously pulled at the label of his Coors Light beer, avoiding eye contact with all the girls in the room whilst clearly simultaneously wishing to steal their attention.

He certainly did not fit the profile of a man that would soon cause the downfall of civilization.

The group had found the quietest corner of the bar and a deck of cards was being shuffled and dealt amongst them. This may be easier than she thought, mused Zara, questioning the need to squeeze herself into this ridiculous plunge bra and short skirt ensemble.

Still, better safe than sorry. Let's get this done, she thought decisively, standing up and sauntering gently over to the table of boys.

'Um, hi guys!' Zara squeaked, the pitch of her voice unnaturally high and girly. 'My girlfriend is running kinda late and the fellas here are making me a bit uncomfortable, do you mind if I sit with you for a bit? What game are you playing?'

Like putty in the hand. Zara had never seen a group of boys suddenly look so excited and frightened at the same time. She gave a little tug of her skirt awkwardly, clutching at her purse tightly to give a vulnerable impression to offset the boldness of her approach. As the boys rushed to make room and collectively explain their overly complex card game, Zara locked eyes with him.

'Hey, I'm Zara,' she said, flashing a sweet smile.

'H...hi...'

It took two years before Zara really went for the jugular. By all accounts, the relationship had been smooth sailing up until then. In retrospect it had been naive of her to assume that just being bendy and making the right noises would be enough to keep his interests for long. As infatuated and distracted by her as he was during these past two years, Zara had started to notice him on his computer more and more, and this was where the danger lay.

On an unassuming Friday night, Zara decided she needed to be a bit more assertive. Whilst care was needed not to sabotage the relationship completely, which would otherwise have made this all for nothing, Zara wanted to snuff this interest in technology out decisively.

After setting the scene with a flurry of opportunistic arguments about her not feeling valued or paid enough attention, Zara went for the big finish.

'I just can't take this anymore – It's me or your damn computer! I'm sorry but I don't want to be with someone who has one eye on me and the other on the monitor all the time. Life is for LIVING! Christ!'

The irony was not lost on Zara, who had in her previous life devoted much of her time to mastering the technology around her. Having to force this issue with such a cliched demand left her feeling slightly disgusted with herself and a very small part of her wanted him to turn around with a backbone and say, *Zara, while you are obviously more important to me than that insignificant machine in the corner, I am deeply concerned that you would end our relationship over something so trivial. I'm afraid this relationship is really going to struggle going forward, not because I'm choosing my hobby over you, but because you've displayed such a lack of respect in giving me this ridiculous ultimatum.*

But he did not say that. And after a short pause he fell to his knees with a heavy sigh and squeezed Zara's leg softly in submission.

'Fine, fine. You are right, Zee, of course it is you. It will always be you. I'll take it all apart tomorrow and be done with it.'

Zara had never really planned on getting married, the concept of everlasting commitment had always unnerved her. She was thankful for the veil providing an illusion of privacy as she reflected on her decisions that had led to this moment.

The year was 2011 and by all accounts her task had been

a success. There would be no way of knowing if she had prevented the world from ending in the long term, as the trip to 2002 was a one-way ticket. But she was hopeful, and through scanning the news each and every morning Zara saw no sign of the destructive path her own world took.

Perhaps she had actually done it, in which case did she really need to still go through with this wedding? She could go off and start a new life in this free and beautiful utopia. Nervous reluctance bubbled up however as she continued down this train of thought. Were she to run away now, it would be into the unknown. There would be no 'mission' to keep her grounded, no direction of travel. No purpose. She would be a woman out of time, with nothing but time on her hands.

But what if she had not achieved her aim yet? And with this the dark clouds of doubt began to creep into her mind, as if welcomed in by the anxiety born of the unknown and straying outside of the comfort zone. Perhaps she needed to stay by his side a little longer, just enough for the youthful flames of entrepreneurship to be extinguished for good.

Zara reassured herself that this was the right decision and hoped that each step down the aisle towards the altar echoed with the confidence she currently lacked.

The priest began his usual spiel, but Zara was only half listening.

'...and do you, Zara Louise Hamilton, take this man to be your lawful wedded husband?'

In for a penny..., thought Zara.

'I do.'

Mark smiled, repeating *I do* at his name as well.

Zara didn't pay too much attention to the rest of the ceremony. She distracted herself with the acknowledgement that her new surname now meant her initials would be 'ZZ'. The alliteration felt like a fictional superhero, and she took a modicum of solace in this idea as they walked down the aisle together to a rainfall of confetti and petals.

Perhaps she had saved the world like the Peter Parkers and Bruce Banners of comic book alum. Her Lex Luther did not point a death ray at the world, however, just created a caustic website and concept that spiralled society out of control. The first innocent domino in a devastating chain. And like the secret identities worn by those fictional heroes, Zara too, would now live on unknown, her contribution to mankind unsung.

At least in this timeline.

GREEN EYES AND HAM

She watched from afar to where that harlot
stood, too close to him to call it innocent.

Her laugh, her touch, that playful nudge tried
to make their connection significant.

In her heart Mary knew her Jacob wouldn't
be tempted by this wretched succubus.

But nonetheless, this burned in her chest,
and she knew she had to be nefarious.

She went on a search for some eye of newt, lav-
ender flowers, and feathers of an owl.

The blood of a pig, a handful of figs
and carcass of fresh waterfowl.

Once in the girl's home Mary scattered the
items around a pot as black as raven.

Then told the village elders of the items found
in a house on the outskirts of Salem.

The trial came quick for the revolting wench who
tried to come between Mary and her betrothed.

They all screamed at the bitch and accused her a witch,
calling for her head just like Mary had hoped.

Across the church she saw Jacob, his face resolute
and her heart brightened at the sight of her lion.

She attempted a wave, though for her efforts was dismayed as his gaze did not leave the sullied siren.

The elders concluded that the girl was guilty
of practicing witchcraft and devilry.

They set her ablaze, the crowd averted their
gaze whilst Mary enjoyed the revelry.

But in horror she watched Jacob jump from the
aisle to embrace the girl upon her lit pyre,

And to Mary's disgust they locked lips in lust
as the two were engulfed in the fire.

The years that followed were unkind to Mary,
whose heart was as broken as bread.

The tramp they called Isabelle and her satanic
spell had tricked Jacob to his death instead.

Unable to cope, she became a recluse in the
same house on the outskirts of Salem.

Plagued by mania she developed necrophilia
and dug up Jacob's corpse just to wed him.

She remained in that gown for the next 44 years,
the white dress turning as black as her sorrow.

The only company she was accustomed
was the corpse of her now husband, a black
cat and the crows of the borough.

Isolated and alone Mary did little but mutter and
sweep as the house surrendered to nature.

The villagers avoided Old Mary's Home, *'It's
haunted,'* whispered children, *'nothing but danger.'*

But then one evening a visitor knocked
and Old Mary cackled with delight.

For before her stood the aura of the man she
had loved and lost on that fateful night.

He was as young and handsome as the day of the trial,
she went to touch his cheek with her old withered hand.

He recoiled from the attempt, she saw the contempt
and then he spoke with a voice sinister yet grand:

*I have come to inform you, old hag, that
this punishment is almost through.*

*You framed my sweet Belle and tried to send her to
hell but instead, that was more deserving of you.*

*As much as you merit this misery and despair,
I have a final gift to help you let go.*

*You accused the wrong crone and spent a life alone
and now it's time to truly reap what you sow.*

With a crack of his fingers Mary saw a white flash
and suddenly found herself out in the dark wood.

She was on all fours, amongst a singular of boars,
in the distance a girl approached in a hood.

Mary recognised the girl as her much younger self,
she tried to shout to stop her ill-fated quest.

But only a squeal was heard as Young Mary walked
towards pulling a knife out from under her breast.

Old Mary knew this scene well, tried to run and
escape but wasn't used to her new piggy feet.

She fell on her snout and again tried to shout
but all Young Mary heard was a bleat.

'The blood of a pig should sort that whore out,' muttered Young Mary as she straddled the swine,

Jacob watched from afar,

as Young Mary stabbed the pig's heart,

blood gushing to the ground

like spilt wine.

THE HOUND AND HARE, CHARING CROSS

15th April 1887

The door to the Hound and Hare swung open and two men shuffled into the dimly lit tavern.

'...And this be her on this inside!' exclaimed the older gentleman in a thick Scottish accent, bitterly removing his sodden raincoat and top hat as he spoke. 'Absolutely disgusting weather, eh? There better be a table free by that there fire.'

'Luckily for us, Derrick,' replied the younger man, looking around the tavern inquisitively, 'it appears not many others have braved the elements this evening.' He continued to survey the scene before him. This was his first time at the Hound and Hare and the stale smell of old beer and tobacco suggested it may also be his last.

The men sat down in front of the fire and got comfortable while the barmaid brought over their drinks. The sound of the howling wind outside caused the old tavern to creak and moan, adding to the symphony of noise produced by the rain pelting on the windows. The drinks arrived at the table just as Derrick was taking off his boots, he flicked a coin at the woman and thanked her.

'Not really the best of times to be giving you a tour of

this wee neck of the woods,' he remarked, staring into the fire longingly. 'You should have come in the summer… but being honest with you, even then this place is hardly a bed of roses to visit Mr… uh…'

'Just Gabe is fine.'

'Gabe… Ah ye poor bastard, your parents never even gave ye a chance with a name like that did they! But then again I can hardly talk!' Derrick laughed heartily as he saw off the rest of his beer, the barmaid brought over another one instinctively. He turned to face her.

'I'll probably be here for a while pet so we can start a tab… I'm giving o' Gabe here a flavour of Charing Cross!' He patted Gabe on the back as he spoke.

Derrick eyed up his new drink, took a gulp and then turned to face his guest.

'So what do you want to know, me boy? Cannee really show you the sights in this weather unfortunately, but I've lived here many a year now so can probably answer any questions you got, it's a book you are writing ye?'

'Yes, a travel book!' replied Gabe enthusiastically. 'I was looking to get some information about the local area and I was pointed in your direction.'

'Ye… well folk know if anyone knows these cobbled streets it be me. Left Glasgow when I was 18 and never looked back!' Derrick explained proudly, throwing more beer down his gullet.

Gabe watched as Derrick finished off his second beer, his own still mostly untouched. He realised he was probably against the clock before Derrick's account would start to become unreliable. He took the pause in the conversation as an opportunity to survey the tavern more closely. Gabe and himself were joined in the tavern by only one other patron, who was sitting in an alcove by the far window. Draped in shadow, the man was only visible by his silhouette against the rain speckled window, a crop of messy long hair and the red glow of his pipe being the only identifiable features.

Unsure if the man in the alcove could see him staring, Gabe turned back to face Derrick.

'So, this place is fairly empty for a Friday night, has the weather put the locals off or are there other watering holes in the area that people go to?'

'Ye… there be a few others, this one is a bit off the beaten path though, so only the true locals come 'ere, very rarely get new folk in.'

'Ah I see,' Gabe replied, pulling some paper out of his coat to make notes. As he jotted down what Derrick had said and he lowered his voice. 'So for instance, that man by the window… another local?'

Derrick did not need to look over. 'Ah ye, that be o' Davey, been coming here years that lad has. Always sits in the dark, the loon, doesn't like to be bothered much so we just leave him be.'

The barmaid arrived with Derrick's third drink as he sat there reflecting quietly for a moment.

''Tis a shame really as he's got some wild stories, I tell ya, haha yeah, they would go good in your wee book!'

'Oh really? What sort?' pressed Gabe.

'Ahh well Davey is a bit away with the fairies so you've gotta take his stories with a pinch o' salt. I tell ya the first time I spoke to him, before I knew he didn't like the company, he went off on a mad one! Entertaining tale mind.'

Gabe looked over at the man in the shadows and back to Derrick, lowering his voice even further so as not to be heard.

'What sort of tale? If you don't mind me asking?'

'Haha! How did I know you'd be asking that? Not really a travel tale but I'll tell ya anyways. Drink up though, lad, before your beer gets warm, the story is a bit of a sitter.'

Gabe took a tentative sip of his beer as requested.

'As Davey tells it…' continued Derrick. 'The circumstances of his sister's death messed him up a bit as a wee lad. He was only eight when she passed, some 20-ish years ago now. Well actually no, I tell a lie, it wasn't her death that caused the trouble, more her funeral.'

'Victoria was 21 when she contracted the plague and survived long enough to see her 22nd birthday. She was a beautiful soul bless 'er and spent many of her days trying to help out the poorer folk around town. A very charitable lass if ever there was one which is why it was such a blow to the whole community when she passed. Her funeral was held at o' Saint Martin-in-the-Fields down the way and everyone in the area turned up to honour her. Very touching for her parents and Davey, there was even a queue out the door and down the road!'

Derrick cleared this throat and finished off his drink. 'Now, this is where Davey's tale goes a bit off the beaten track.

'Some time into the ceremony, a stranger pushed his way past the crowd and began to walk up amongst the pews. Davey describes him as a tall fella, his cloak an array of black feathers with a top hat to match. The sound of his footsteps echoed around the church, to the point that the poor priest had to stop what he was saying. It was at this point the crowd started to pay more notice to the man, who, as he made his way up the aisle, looked like he was laughing.

'Davey says at this point his pa shot up and grabbed the man by the neck, telling him to have some respect for the dead and to leave. The laughing man took no notice apparently and pushed Davey's pa, a big lad mind, off him with an effortless flick of his hand. Everyone looked on as the man approached Victoria's coffin, leaping up to sit on top of it and face the stunned crowd. The laughing man then began to speak with a cold, sharp voice as he looked around the church before him: "*Quite the popular girl this one, it seems.*" Davey's ma started to sob, his pa picked himself up from the floor and ran at the man again, his face full o' rage. The laughing man looked on in amusement, his eyes following Davey's pa with a sort of hunger. Suddenly, behind the laughing man, uncoiled some kind of… well tail, Davey says, that speared towards his pa, wrapping around his neck, and stopping him in his tracks.'

Derrick looked up at the barmaid who had arrived at the table to clear his drink away.

'Can we get a bowl of nuts also please, pet?'

'You're not boring this poor boy with your tales are you, Dee?' asked the Barmaid playfully.

'He asked! He asked… and they be Davey's tales I be telling.'

'Oh… lucky him,' she said dryly, rolling her eyes, 'a load of old tosh the lot of it. Himself is in a foul old mood tonight anyway so make sure he don't hear you telling it wrong!'

'What and leave his brooding spot? That'd be the day, lass.' They shared a chuckle and the barmaid shuffled off to fetch the nuts.

'Right where was I?' Derrick muttered.

'Something about a man with a… tail? I believe?' said Gabe slowly. Derrick laughed.

'Oh, right you are, well this man, currently sitting on top of poor Victoria's coffin, was apparently the Devil himself!'

Derrick waited a beat before continuing, his eyebrows raised and a smile on his face in incredulity. He was a natural storyteller, Gabe admitted to himself, responding in turn to Derrick's pause and facial expression with a look of confusion and bewilderment of his own.

'Aye you heard me right, lad, the Devil! So, he's just

subdued Davey's pa by some supernatural means and the crowd in the church start to scream and flee. Somehow, the doors fly shut, trapping the good 50 or so men and women inside the church, Davey and his family included. Now I cannot really remember where he goes with this next, something about the Devil doing a dramatic speech on top of his sister's coffin when all of a sudden – BAM!'

Derrick slapped on the table excitedly. 'A beam of light bursts through the church's roof, hitting the middle of the aisle just to the right of Davey. On the floor inside this light knelt a familiar figure, Victoria! Sent from the heavens she was. She rose from the floor adorned in white robes with majestic wings flexing behind her as she stood, the staff in her hand was raised and pointed threateningly at the man atop her coffin. The Devil, flared with anger, spoke in a tongue not known to Davey, hissing as he recoiled from the light in front of him, insatiable rage painted on his face, tail lashing around him aggressively, rearing to face Victoria's staff.

'But then she spoke, in the same language he had heard the Devil spit just before. But this time it was like a pacifying wave, her words muting the screams and wails from around the church. The Devil was clearly responding, but his voice could be heard no longer. A tranquillity had filled the room and Victoria took the moment to look around the church at those who had come to mourn her. As her gaze passed over her family, a sad smile flashed across her face. It was visible only for a fleeting second, before an immense white light exploded from her staff, blinding them all.

'As the light faded, everything was as it was before. The priest was finishing his eulogy and Davey's ma and pa were besides him, watching the service silently. No Devil, no Victoria, no nothing, it was as if it all didn't happen. Except Davey knew different. Only he came out of that church

with memories of the Devil dancing on his sister's coffin...
to everyone else... David's story is a child's fantasy.'

The peanuts had arrived at the table and Derrick grabbed a handful, smiling at Gabe broadly.

'See I told ye it was a wild one! Davey tells it much better than I do mind. It's a shame o' Casper Clatterby isn't in here tonight, I tell ya that, lad, Casp was actually at Victoria's funeral that day and didn't see a dickie bird about folk in black feathers or any of that rubbish.' Derrick washed down the nuts with some beer, shaking his head.

'Poor Davey... the lengths our minds can go to when dealing with grief eh?'

The topic changed and Derrick and Gabe continued to drink long into the night.

At 10 past 2 in the morning, Derrick finally slumped onto the table in a drunken stupor, his tales of Charing Cross petering into incoherence. The fire in front of the men crackled quietly, a sound only audible now that the rain had tempered.

At the sound of Derrick's snores, Gabe rose sharply to his feet and made his way towards the window where the man in the alcove still sat. As he neared, the shadows spoke.

'You took your time to approach, Gabriel.'

Gabriel sat without invitation, letting out a frustrated sigh.

'I couldn't risk my new friend over there seeing me come over. Unfortunately, he had a far greater resilience to that ghastly stuff than I had appreciated.'

'Well, Derrick is a very seasoned patron, it was entertaining to watch... apart from having to hear the name "Davey" over and over...'

'Listen, David, I am glad to have finally found you but having to indulge in tonight's charade for so long has left us little time for pleasantries.'

David sat forward to tap the ash out of his pipe. He was briefly illuminated by the light of the tavern and Gabriel could see many scars littered across his face, a fresh cut running down below his eye. David leaned back into the darkness, his eyes focused on the street outside the window.

'Gabriel, it is never good news when you seek me out, which is why I go through such efforts to not be found.'

'While that may be so, this is important. Victoria has gone missing.'

The shadows did not move. David pondered his response carefully, his eyes moving back to meet Gabriel's.

'She is very capable of looking after herself,' he said plainly, 'and you lot are quite hardy... from my experience.'

Gabriel ignored the comment and withdrew a piece of paper from his overcoat. 'This is a ticket to Cairo, Egypt. This is where I believe Victoria to have travelled.'

'Cairo? Why would she go to Cairo?'

Gabriel paused before continuing, he leant in closer to David and spoke hurriedly.

'There are dark forces in Egypt, David, raw and unstable forces. In the months before her disappearance Victoria became increasingly interested in Cairo, devoting much of our resources to observing the whispers and movements within the city.' He sighed. 'Nobody knows where Victoria has gone. Many have come to me as Second in Command to ask where she could have gone and frankly the first place I would look is Cairo.'

David scratched his chin slowly, taking the pause to process Gabriel's information. He looked up at Gabriel, the playfulness in his voice now gone.

'Why seek me then, Gabriel? Heaven has countless men and women who would be honoured to find favour in your good books by locating Victoria.'

'I could tell you it's because your mortality affords you

unrestricted access to the areas and lands forbidden to my kind…' reasoned Gabriel, who sighed heavily again as he looked from David to the street outside the window. 'The reality is though… with Victoria missing, many up top are worried that this could be a sign of another great war on the horizon. I am sure you are more than aware that the tension is dangerously fragile once again. With Victoria gone, it's my responsibility to keep order until more facts are known – flooding the streets of Cairo with white wings will only cause chaos.' Gabriel paused before adding, 'Plus, she is your sister, I would have thought…'

'Oh don't start up with that, Gabriel,' flared David irritably.

Gabriel's reply was careful, but stern.

'…Troubled as your relationship may be, were she to be in your shoes right now, this boat ticket would certainly not be laying here on the table untouched…'

Not to Gabriel's surprise, David slapped his hand down on the table angrily and dragged the ticket towards him, bitterly stuffing it into his overcoat pocket.

Gabriel stood up cheerfully.

'Great – I must dash before the barmaid spots me here. A woman called Naxxus will greet you in Cairo, as part of the patrol leading Victoria's excursions there, she is an excellent place to start.'

David's focus was on refilling his pipe, somewhat aggressively.

'Mmmm. Goodbye then, Gabriel, lovely to see you as always,' he muttered sarcastically.

'Likewise,' Responded Gabriel briskly, turning to leave. As he passed the comatose figure near the fire, he touched an exposed arm gently, causing the man to bolt up in shock and confusion.

'Derrick, it's me Gabe, you drifted off. Let's get you home to your wife, shall we?'

'…Euuughh yyyes, lad that be bests…' slurred Derrick, picking himself up with a wobble and leaning on Gabriel as they staggered out of The Horse and Hare.

14th April 1887

The door to the Hound and Hare creaked open to reveal a well-dressed gentleman standing tentatively on the street outside, peeking before the threshold of the dimly lit tavern and reviewing the inside before deciding it was not his scene. The door fell closed as shyly as it had opened.

'Aye we don't want your sort in 'ere anyway, lad,' growled a low Scottish voice from a patron sitting at the bar.

At the back of the room, David sat accompanied only by the shadows of the alcove. The ale before him was mostly untouched and flakes of burnt tobacco peppered the table. What little light that could penetrate the darkness skipped onto the surfaces with a rich orange and pink hue. With a glance to the damaged window adjacent to him, David noticed the day was finally drawing in and that meant he had somewhere he needed to be. With a concluding swig of the now lukewarm ale, David stood to his feet and headed to the tavern door with purpose. The tails of his overcoat licked at his heels as he grabbed the top hat that hung from the peg by the door, becoming a black silhouette against the low evening sun as he strode down the cobbled path towards Jacob's Barbers.

The warlock Jacob was one of David's more familiar faces in the city. Although Jacob dabbled in the sin of the Devil and much wished for his contemporaries to see him as a dangerous and intimidating mage, his prowess in mastering the dark arts left much to be desired. Except for a few locals whose hair appeared to grow unnaturally thick and fast,

Jacob's nefarious impact on this world was very minimal and his lowly status within the ranks of the Damned meant he was the perfect person to lean on for a bit of information.

As the bell above the entrance announced David's arrival at the barbers, he braced himself for Jacob's undoubtably warm and excited greeting.

'Oh fucking hell,' Jacob muttered, aggressively sweeping fallen hair into a pile before leaning his broom against the wall. He turned to David and crossed his arms. 'You are a plague, David, your visits cost me customers. Is there not some other honest establishment you can bother relentlessly?'

'There must be some sort of spell you can cast to clean this mess up rather than manually sweeping…' David mused, kneeling to feign interest in the floor and ignoring Jacob's question. 'Or is it more for a celebration of the art that you sweep this floor with such care, Jacob?'

'Wow, fantastic idea, why didn't I think of that?' Jacob retorted dryly. 'I'll just go and get that "Spells-for-cleaning-up-the-floor" book from out the back and get to it, what a brilliant insight thank you.' Jacob rolled his eyes before stomping behind the counter as if the exchange of rhetorical questions would conclude the visit.

David contemplated challenging him to get this clearly non-existent book from the back but decided against it. He needed cooperation from Jacob today and snappy little jibes at his expense were not going to help him.

'Anyway, I'm here for a shave,' he announced merrily, standing to his feet, as if oblivious to the tone of Jacob's words.

Jacob groaned, but a fleeting glance to the somewhat lacking penny jar on the counter told David that he had timed his visit just right.

'Fine, fine,' Jacob muttered reluctantly. 'If it means you

will leave me in peace then I can squeeze you in quickly now.'

'Superb!' bounced David.

'But just a shave, in silence. You then pay, also in silence, and then you are gone, again, silently.'

'Of course, of course, of course,' David said, nodding happily as he lowered himself into the barber's chair. 'I'm just here for the o' cheeks and chin.'

'Good, because it's been a really long day and the last thing I need is...'

'...Yeah just here for a shave...' David interrupted casually, looking around as he reclined, '...a shave and a chat.'

Jacob sighed.

There was a distinct lack of care in the manner in which shaving cream was being applied onto his face, thought David, almost as if Jacob was in a rush.

'I'm not interrupting anything am I?' David asked, blowing away the cream from his lips.

'You are always interrupting,' responded Jacob, curtly.

A brief silence followed, David decided to see if Jacob would fill it himself.

'...If this is about the incident down Barrows Court last week, I had nothing to do with it. I don't even use pentagrams, that is not my style at all.'

'I am not here about poor Mrs Jessops.'

David felt the cold edge of Jacob's blade rest upon his neck momentarily before being dragged upwards and away.

'Okay good, I mean, if you were here for that, I would not have much to say anyway...'

Another pause lingered. David wondered if Jacob would fill this one also.

'...Other than I do know that Joseph Kettermen down

Stokes Way was recently bragging about obtaining an old ram's skull…'

'Mmmmm,' considered David, 'One for the authorities I think.'

With the neck now clean, Jacob moved the blade and pressed it firmly against his cheek.

'Despite the gossip, Mrs Jessops looks to have died of blunt force trauma rather than anything more sinister. But it is good to know about Joseph and his affinity for the macabre, one to keep an eye on.'

Finishing the first, Jacob now moved the knife over the other cheek, dragging the hairs away once again.

'But no,' David continued, 'I am here regarding the appointment you had with Gabriel yesterday.'

The question clearly caught Jacob by surprise, so much so that the sudden distraction caused his blade to nick David just below his eye. A small mound of blood swelled from its centre.

'I… erm, sorry for that,' mumbled Jacob clumsily, looking for a rag around him.

'Ignore it.' David sat up to face him, wiping the blood away with his fingers, his voice now stern. 'Why was Gabriel here, Jacob?'

The warlock met his gaze, appearing to choose his words carefully.

'He wasn't.'

'Then why is there Angel hair on your floor?'

They both looked down to where David had inspected the floor upon arrival, the silver strands stood out clear against the mottled brown.

'Well, that's quite simple…' Jacob stalled for thought. 'Because….'

'Because it was one of the other Angels you mean to tell me? Archangel Michael perhaps? With his bald, shiny head.

Or Archangel Raphael, who would not let the Lord himself touch his long, luscious locks let alone some back-alley barbers.'

The two men stared at each other for a beat, David persisted.

'The Angels are often careful about being seen down here, I need not remind you of the strict rules they must abide by, which makes it all the more compelling why Gabriel would run such a risk.'

Jacob sighed, beaten.

'He was here, Gabriel, yeah, he was after you.'

'Did he say why?'

'Only that is was to do with your sister, gone missing or words to that effect.'

'Mmmm,' considered David again, reclining back into the chair in thought. 'Did you tell him where I was?'

'No,' replied Jacob, finishing up the shave with much more care than he had previously. 'But I told him he would likely find you in the Hound and Hare tomorrow night.'

'A bit presumptuous if you ask me...' mumbled David as Jacob cleaned up the last of the shaving cream. 'Rarely do the Angels seek the help of the Damned, why did he come to you?'

'I'm not one to pry,' lied Jacob, 'but it appeared to me Gabriel did not want many to know about his search for you, at least, that was what I read into from his overly generous payment for a haircut.'

David appeared too distracted to respond to this however, as he had found another of Gabriel's hairs stuck to the chair next to him. He picked it up and to Jacob's astonishment, the hair coiled in David's hand, a red mist evaporating off them.

'I had heard the rumours...' Jacob started, mesmerised, 'but never believed them to be true. Is that how you can see and interact with the supernatural?'

David looked back to him, only half listening. Jacob motioned towards the cut on his cheek and then to his hand where he had wiped the blood away.

'It's your blood, right? That's how you do what you do... hey what is going on with you? You look spooked.'

'I'm fine.' David was eyeing the strand of hair carefully. 'I just don't like blood. Listen, what would you say if I offered you to join me on an errand to Cairo?'

Jacob was understandably taken aback from the abrupt change in topic.

'Cairo? What is in Cairo? And more importantly why would I go with you?'

'I am in need of someone with your particular skill set, Jacob,' Responded David, a sentence that usually would carry an air of sarcasm to it when talking to Jacob. Not today however. 'I will pay handsomely for your time away from this fine and bustling establishment.'

Jacob frowned and looked at David sceptically.

'How handsomely is handsomely? I certainly don't enjoy your company enough to do it for cheap, or even moderate payment.'

'You'll have to trust me,' said David, flatly. 'I have a ticket to Cairo already and I have a sneaking suspicion I will have another in my possession by tomorrow night.'

'Well, I don't trust you, so that's the first thing, it'll be cash up front, but more importantly, how do you already have a ticket to Cairo? Let alone a second on its way apparently. Those things cost a fortune.'

'I got the first one from Victoria.'

Jacob scrunched up his face in confusion.

'Your sister? What – When? I thought she was missing?'

'Last night. Yes it's a rather complex picture, are you expecting any more clients after me?'

'No...'

'So much for "squeezing me in" then,' scoffed David, motioning for Jacob to take a seat as he flipped the door's 'Open' sign to 'Close'.

'Please, take a pew and I will explain, there are a few moving parts to this that you will need to be privy to if we are going to holiday together.'

13th April 1887

The door to the Hound and Hare remained shut. The bell for last orders reverberated around the room like a siren, startling the inebriated and angering those not quite there yet.

All but two. Those that dwelled in the dark shadows of the alcove spoke in hushed tones, too absorbed in their conversation to notice.

'... It can't be that serious, Victoria,' dismissed David, thumbing tobacco into his pipe as he spoke.

'Consider what other possible reason there would be for me to meet you here, in this... *establishment,* against protocol.'

Victoria had not aged a day. Frozen in time with the same natural beauty that she radiated all those years ago, matured only by the manner of which she now spoke. The years spent at the helm of the Lord's Messengers adding an air of wisdom and experience that did befit the face of a 22-year-old woman.

David found interactions with his sister slightly unnerving for this reason, fortunately for him their paths seldom crossed.

'I'm afraid I'm going to need more information.'

'You have the information you need: the Heavens are in trouble and you need to position yourself into a more favourable situation for when the fallout hits.' Victoria clasped her glass as she spoke, but did not take a sip.

'What do you mean a *more favourable situation?*' David retorted, knowing full well what she meant by those words.

'You are hardly allied to either side in this war, and yet a considerable amount of your energy seems to be on being a nuisance to both.'

David winced in annoyance.

'It is called being neutral, just because someone has white wings does not mean they...'

'Oh, save me the speech, David,' interrupted Victoria. 'You are a mere mercenary, don't delude yourself that there is some philosophical message to your life choices. Your morals clearly bend for whoever pays you the most.'

A tense silence followed Victoria's barbed exchange. She had expected David to come back with some sort of witty retort, but instead he flashed his eyebrows and sat back into his seat, the shadows obscuring most of his face.

Victoria did not have the time for these theatrics and quarrels, this could potentially be the last time she saw her brother. After taking a deep breath, she broke the silence.

'You were *going* to say that just because someone has white wings doesn't mean they are right? I presume? Or good?'

It was a rhetorical question that David did not need to answer, Victoria was staring intently at her glass, running her fingers along the grooves absent-mindedly, considering her next words carefully. '...And you would be right either way. It appears that a halo can be deceiving.'

David could sense the change in the tone of conversation and sat forward carefully as if not to scare it away.

'What has happened, Victoria?' he said, cautiously concerned.

'Heaven will likely fall, David,' responded Victoria, flatly. 'We have lost.'

'You need to give me more than that.' He placed a gentle hand atop Victoria's busy hand. It was cold, not nearly as pleasant as one would assume touching an Angel to be. It felt the same as it had done when he held her hand the day he discovered her body. He had held it tighter that day to try and warm her up, and without thinking, he was squeezing it tighter again too.

Victoria placed her free hand atop David's and savoured what was a rare and human moment for her. Disarmed, she sighed.

'An incident yesterday revealed that Heaven has been infiltrated by the Damned, specifically, they have somehow figured out how to corrupt the Angels.'

'How can you be sure? To my knowledge all the attempts to turn the Angels have always failed?'

Victoria shook her head bitterly.

'We were investigating reports of powerful forces in Cairo, Egypt. I had sent Naxxus and Uriel, two of our best, with a small cohort to report on what they observed there while Gabriel, Michael, Raphael and myself observed from the clouds.

'Our oversight of Cairo was limited and as the group passed into the shadow of a pyramid, our ability to communicate with them was cut.'

David nodded.

'...Not an uncommon trick of the Damned,' he said, letting Victoria continue.

'No. Despite the troubles in reaching the team, a prayer did reach us eventually. It was fragmented and difficult to understand at first, but Gabriel deciphered it, it was a cry for help.'

'From one of the Angels? Why?'

'Yes, from Uriel, he was injured. The prayer had said that Naxxus had turned on them the moment they were inside the pyramid and he was gravely hurt.'

David was taken aback, his previous interactions with

Naxxus gave the impression she was one of the more pious of the Angels.

'*Naxxus*? Really?' he said incredulously.

'Let me finish,' Victoria responded, holding up a hand to prevent further interruption. 'We sent a team down as soon as Gabriel deciphered the message to pick up Naxxus and the slain, bringing Naxxus in front of myself and the Archangels for questioning.'

'She was bought in shackled and bound, but I saw no more evil on her than I did before, and this concerned me. I approached cautiously to talk to her, to try and understand all this, which is when she gave me this.'

Victoria pulled her robes aside to reveal a fresh stab wound glistening just below her ribs to the side.

'Now this is where the story gets interesting,' assured Victoria, concealing her injury once again.

'The chaos around Naxxus attacking me revealed a few things, it was such a blur of activity that it would have been easy to miss. Firstly, her chains had not been locked or tightened, it was just an illusion of captivity.'

David was losing the thread of this story.

'Wait, wait, so she was bought in with the intention of attacking you? Who was the guard with her?'

Victoria's hand of interruption returned but she nodded in acknowledgement of his question.

'The guard was in fact Uriel in disguise. We had paid no attention to him once Naxxus was bought before us, so that amongst the commotion of the attack he was able to act.'

'*Gravely injured* Uriel from the pyramid?' responded David, incredulously.

'The very same. But this is where the real information resides – it would soon transpire that Naxxus and Uriel were in fact performing this façade for the greater good. Their investigation of the pyramid discovered the existence of a mole within the Court of Angels. Knowing that relaying this information back would spook the traitor, they orchestrated this elaborate plan to ensure they could be in the same room when they revealed their findings.'

'Incredible, so Naxxus and Uriel were not actually corrupt? What about when she stabbed you?'

'You are aware, are you not, of the power our blood has at revealing the true nature of a being?' responded Victoria. 'Naxxus was, the attack was meant to spill just enough of my blood to be used to identify the traitor but do no lasting damage to myself. As the blade was flung behind Naxxus on its way out of me, my blood was cast across the room. It was for Uriel to watch how our fellow brethren reacted to this.'

'And how did they react?'

'Gabriel propelled Naxxus away from me immediately with his staff and pinned her against the wall, while Michael ran over to assist me on the floor. It was, however, quite clear from Raphael's response that he did not wish to get too close to me, nor the blood adorning the floor. Revealing himself, Uriel restrained Raphael and barked for Gabriel to release Naxxus. The truth eventually came forth.'

David sat back again, this time not for dramatic effect but for the sheer volume of information he had just had to process. It was hard to believe that Raphael could be in league with the Damned.

After a short pause, David spoke.

'What happened to Raphael? How long has he been working for the Devil do you know?'

'We don't know. He disputed Naxxus and Uriel's story for a short while but eventually gave up and tried to flee, screaming that the house of the Lord was tainted and must fall. The usual expletives. He resides in the stockades for now... I am not sure what to do with him in all honesty.'

'From my experience it is hard to keep an Angel captive for long,' reflected David. 'But why are you here? It sounds as if the Angels need your leadership more than ever now.'

Victoria shook her head.

'I let my guard down, David. It was under my watch that one of my command was able to infiltrate the Court. Lord knows how much sensitive information he was able to pass to the Damned,' she said, deflated.

'I am here to alert you of the changes afoot and to potentially say goodbye for the last time. I am to travel to Cairo myself to discover what is exactly happening there and if any more can be revealed about this clandestine campaign of the Damned to get into Heaven.'

'Are you under the impression there could be more corruption then?' queried David.

'Potentially, until I get to the bottom of it, I can't really trust anyone, apart from, bizarrely, you.'

It was David's turn to shake his head.

'This seems impractical, Victoria. There are certain limitations on how you can travel, you will not be able to get to Cairo without being detected. And then what will you do? At a time when suspicion amongst the white wings must be at an all-time high you don't really want to be caught sneaking into the enemy's camp.'

Victoria did not say anything at first and looked around the patrons of the tavern slowly migrating towards the door to leave.

'…I must go soon,' she said softly.

'Listen.' David grabbed her cold hand again. 'Let us think about this logically. You going to Cairo could potentially be a trap, there is something going on with all of this and walking into the belly of the beast unprepared is not the answer. Does anyone know your intentions to travel to Cairo other than me?'

'Gabriel will likely figure it out,' conceded Victoria.

'And you have a ticket already?'

'I do.'

'Perfect, this is what we will do. I will go to Cairo in your place. I suggest you take refuge with the Valkyrie or something and I'll contact you when I know more.'

'I can't ask you to do that, David.'

'You aren't. I am telling you that is what I am doing.'

The two stared at each other for a moment, before Victoria nodded softly.

'What you propose makes sense. The Valkyrie has always been an ally to us and perhaps taking a more cautious approach here is best until we know a bit more.'

From across the room, they noticed the barmaid snuffing out the lanterns on the tables from around the room, ebbing closer to the alcove which they occupied. Victoria placed her now empty glass to the side, ready to depart.

'I'll await your word in Norway then,' she concluded.

'Wait, wait before you go,' David spluttered, noticing Victoria beginning to stand. 'What would have happened if Raphael had touched your blood? I have used my own many times to uncover followers of the Damned, but never an Angel. It may be handy in Cairo.'

Victoria thought for a second.

'I have only used my blood once on a fellow Angel, and that was during the Trial of Lucifer. Under normal conditions, our blood has no impact on someone pure of heart. But in the case of Lucifer, and I assume Raphael had he have gotten close enough, contact with the blood exposes the evil of the Devil in a person's heart, releasing a dark red mist from where it touched and alerting those looking on that their soul has been corrupted.'

'Noted,' David said, cautious of the approaching barmaid. 'Can I walk you out?'

'It is best you don't. I will look for your word, David, thank you... for this... and please, take care.'

'We will sort this out, Victoria,' David said reassuringly. He went to say more, but a loud voice from the other side of the room tore through the quiet atmosphere of the alcove.

'Eerrrrr, Davey it's kick out, pet, c'mon lad, who you talkin' to anyway?'

'...Just myself, Derrick,' responded David, looking back to the now empty pew opposite him.

David picked up a small rectangular piece of paper that lay just to the right of his pipe and hat. A boat ticket to Cairo. Collecting his things, David thanked the barmaid for taking his glass and turned to leave the Hound and Hare.

ABJECTNATION

'Abjectnation is not a real word,' hissed Rose, growing tired of both the argument and the Scrabble game.

'It is,' puffed Matt, defiantly. 'If you can have *Expelliarmus* then I can have *Abjectnation*.'

'Expelliarmus is in the Harry Potter books though.'

'So, if Abjectnation was in a book it would be allowed?'

'I guess, but it isn't! Take those tiles off *please*!'

'Hold on,' teased Matt, running to the study giddily. 'You are not going to believe this…'

IT'S NOT THE END OF THE WORLD

Graham lay awake trying to ignore the screams coming from a patient in the room adjacent.

His attention was focused on a small fly crawling across the ceiling, seemingly indifferent to the shrill noise disturbing the otherwise peaceful silence. The fly was clumsily making its way towards the open window near where Graham lay, probably attracted to the cold gusts of wind which pierced through the stuffy air inside.

Graham sighed softly, he looked curiously at the fly one last time before sitting up to look outside his window.

The hospital's grounds were vacant, moonlight revealing only a handful of cars in the whole car park, all of which had been abandoned haphazardly in no specific space. In the distance the lights of the city sparkled above the treeline, an aura of warm yellow rose into the black sky above it like an artificial sunrise. The city wasn't far away, but the difference in activity made it feel like a distant shore.

Graham's attention was aggressively stolen away from the horizon by a sharp rattling noise below. Three men could be seen running out of the hospital with an overfilled shopping trolley, boxes of medicine falling to the ground in their wake as they scampered across the car park, eventually disappearing into the treeline. No one was chasing them, and no one would, it was the fifth time Graham had seen it happen this week.

'There can't be much more left to plunder surely,' growled Graham. He wasn't really sure if he was speaking to the fly or just himself, but talking out loud made him feel less alone.

Graham reached into his dressing gown pocket and pulled out a weathered box of cigarettes, lazily placing one between his lips and letting it hang loosely as he picked up the lighter from the bedside table. As he lit it, the flame's reflection in the window caught his attention and he met his own gaze. He looked old and tired. His long dark hair was looking greasy and peppered with grey hairs, much like his unkempt stubble. The reflection was a stark reminder of how much he had aged in the last couple of years.

He let out another sigh and focused back on the city, no doubt the last couple of weeks will have taken their toll too.

The world had changed quite drastically in a very short period of time. It was only a fortnight ago when Graham first saw the colossal prism hovering above Oxford. He had watched it in awe as it slowly descended beyond the city's skyline and out of his sight.

In utter disbelief and shock, he switched on the news to find out what was going on, half expecting and hoping this to just be a side effect of his medicine. The structure, a stadium sized perfect metallic grey prism, was not a hallucination, or at least one that the local news was playing along with, and had planted itself neatly in the middle of one of the cities park's by 3pm that day. There were no casualties, although if you were to ask the man who left his bike in the park as he ran away from the prism, his crushed property should be considered a casualty.

We weren't alone in the universe it seemed, and rather than us discovering alien life on another planet like was always the expectation, it had found us instead. The following days were filled with worldwide hysteria, intrigue and, most destructively, fear.

Had the structure just appeared and everything else stayed the same, society, would have probably been able to cope. We had, to some degree, prepared psychologically for a moment like this through Hollywood's historic obsession with extra-terrestrial media.

As to be expected, the initial frenzy caused by the appearance of the structure changed the very foundations of people's beliefs worldwide, unifying religion and science in an equal challenge to their understanding of the universe. Shaken as the world was, at least as a civilisation, it remained... for a short period of time at least. Glued to his only access to the outside world, Graham watched on the television as the appearance of the structure started to rally the world into a period of peace.

Governments from around the world, even former adversaries, sent scientists and resources to the United Kingdom to help study the structure over the following days. The world put almost everything aside to form solidarity with each other in a time of uncertainty, aggressive territorial ambitions and old grudges were all put into perspective by this new shiny object in Oxford, England.

Unfortunately, but predictably, this new world did not last.

In the 12 days following the arrival of 'The Visitor', as coined by the media, scientists were no closer to understanding... anything really. The structure was made of a metal, that much was clear, but no other information as to where it came from, how it achieved aviation or its purpose on Earth was discovered.

Frustrations and paranoia were beginning to seep into the minds of the people and the site of the structure was dogged with aggressive protests. A paranoid vocal minority started to question whether this was a hoax, distracting us from the 'real news' and animosity between the people and the UK government started to grow, somewhat spurred on by foreign countries embittered that the structure hadn't chosen to settle in their land instead.

In other areas of the world, tensions erupted. Religious countries clashed from within and against each other, some wanted to worship The Visitor as the second coming of Christ while others wanted to denounce it as a false god and destroy it. All debates and disagreements were all quashed, however, at the arrival of 'The Countdown' on the 12th day.

Exactly 288 hours after the structure touched down on the soft grass of South Park, Graham's television switched off without warning while he was sleeping. The sudden lack of ambient noise woke him up to an unusually dark room. He grabbed the remote next to him and tapped all the usual buttons. Nothing. Tired and exasperated, he crawled to the end of his bed to check the plug and its connection to the television suspended above. Still nothing.

Annoyance was setting in, the television was his only outlet to the world outside this hospital and, without it, he would not know what was going on. With a disgruntled exhale of breath, Graham had moodily grabbed the dressing gown next to him and slipped into the wheelchair next to his bed. He did not socialise with the other patients that much, his tolerance for their meaningless chat dwindled long ago. He spoke very occasionally however to an elderly patient called Bertie down the hall. Knowing that Bertie rarely slept anyway, Graham wanted to see if he was having similar electrical problems.

As Graham reached his door, a bright blue glow burst into the room behind him. Alarmed, he wheeled around and looked back to see his screen suddenly illuminated. The relief he felt was short lived as it quickly became clear that the television was not showing anything remotely like BBC News anymore. He cautiously crept closer to get a better look.

On the screen now appeared a set of bright blue symbols, the most beautiful and mesmerising symbols he had ever seen in his life. Graham gazed upon the screen like he was discovering a brand-new colour. The symbols were intoxicating, a melody of lines and complex shapes, some familiar and some new. Graham felt tears rolling down his cheeks. He watched as the blue lights contorted, twisted and flowed over the screen like a work of art, he was sure no sound was coming from the television but at the same time felt like a symphony was playing around him in time to the symbol's movements.

After an unknown period of time, Graham realised that, beyond the beauty of these strange symbols, he could actually understand what they were conveying. They were just numbers; just written in a different language that he somehow could now read. He could make out an 11, a 23 and a third set of numbers that was changing periodically. The sudden reminder of something familiar snapped him back to reality. It appeared to be a countdown to something in just under 12 days' time. But to what?

Graham wiped his eyes and tried to collect his thoughts, his mind racing. Abruptly, he made his way to the window, hoisted himself onto his bed and looked along at the hospital building. All the windows were illuminated with a similar soft blue glow. The sound of doors opening in the hallway outside told Graham other patients were also confused, Bertie's voice could then be heard.

'What the bloody hell is going on now?'

Almost the full 12 days had passed since the countdown first appeared. Graham closed his eyes and drew in the smoke from his cigarette, softly blowing it out of a gap in the window where it danced in an invisible current. The fly had reached the window now and was trying to get through the invisible barrier, which was the glass, clearly eager to soar in the night's cold air.

Even from his solitary room in the hospital, Graham could tell the world outside these walls no longer represented the one he knew, and he found a sense of morbid humour in the fact that it had taken less than a month for modern life to collapse completely. After talking to the other patients on that first night, Graham discovered that alongside televisions, all computers and mobile phones were also disabled, only useful for displaying the mysterious countdown.

The only form of information anyone could receive was initially through radio, however, after a week the radio waves slowly fell silent, with just the soft crackle of feedback being heard on every channel.

In the days following the start of the countdown, madness had apparently swept through the world. Fearing the timer and the uncertainty around its purpose, the majority of people stopped going to work to spend time with their family. Some people rushed to fulfil the dreams they always thought they had time for, whereas others took to the streets in gangs to vent their anger and to feel in control.

The radio told stories of rapes and murders becoming rampant throughout the country, urging women and men to stay in groups and in safe, well lit, locations. Shops were looted for food and luxury goods, although ironically television and computer stores were mostly left untouched this time.

Scientists had now stopped examining the structure in South Park, it had become too dangerous to be around that area with many people taking their frustrations out on The Visitor. The Army tried to keep control of the population and to some degree it appeared like they had succeeded, Graham frequently saw helicopters above the city with the occasional tank convoy rolling past the hospital towards it, there was no way of knowing if their efforts were working, however.

The military leaders eventually decided that the radio stations were detrimental to the peace they were trying to keep, so they shut them down in an attempt to stop the fear spreading. The last transmission heard was two days ago. The host frantically gave the listeners the latest areas where gangs had been spotted just as gunshots pierced through the radio speakers. It was unclear whether he had been targeted by military or someone less savoury. Either way, the radio waves were now silent.

Reactions to the situation on Graham's ward differed quite substantially to that of the general population, it appeared. People were only here because of a terminal illness of some sorts, and in contrast to probably the rest of the planet, were optimistic and looking forward to the countdown. Some fantasised about it being the rapture to Heaven, while others dreamt that it was the arrival of alien life that could heal them of their sickness. Being amongst all the positivity in the ward while the world destroyed itself around it felt surreal, like being in the eye of a storm. Most nights on the ward were filled with laughter and games, as some of earth's unluckiest souls found happiness and excitement while the world collapsed around them.

Graham did not contribute to the jovial atmosphere. He knew his presence amongst the others bought the mood down for them, so he continued to keep himself to himself for the most part. As the days progressed, the number of doctors and nurses in the unit dwindled and as a result the less healthy patients could not cope with the drop in care. He could not remember the last time he saw Bertie but presumed the worst. Graham now rarely left his room except to collect food from the mess room.

His self-imposed exile was briefly interrupted on the night before last. He was rolling back towards his room with his dinner tray on his lap when his journey was interrupted. Some families of the patients on the ward had moved into the hospital to be closer to their relatives at this confusing time. This included Little Lucy, whose energy and excitement was often at odds with the drab atmosphere surrounding her.

'G, G! What do you think will happen at the end of the countdown?' she had asked hopefully, clearly oblivious to the attempts of her family trying to approach her.

Graham stopped his chair and looked over Lucy's shoulder to the group she had been a part of. All of them were watching with trepidation and uncertainty as to how Graham would respond.

Lucy continued to talk animatedly through the silence.

'…I think The Visitor will open up and be a spaceship to take us all to another planet and it will fit everyone in and we will all have a great big party on the way!' she said, beaming. 'Thomas doesn't though, he thinks it will be a bomb and Daddy won't say what he thinks, I don't want to believe that though, what about you?'

An older man, presumably Lucy's father, came over to the two of them. 'Lucy? Lucy my love… I'm not sure Mr Castle wants to play our little game of What Ifs, let's go back to table and let him go on his way shall we?'

Graham looked from Lucy to the man and back again, disappointment appearing on the younger girl's face. 'Oh, alright then…' Lucy mumbled dejectedly as she turned to walk back towards the group.

'Lucy?'

Both Lucy and the man spun around. It occurred to Graham that neither had probably heard him speak before, explaining their shocked expression.

'I hope there will be room for my wheelchair at the spaceship party later.' he said quietly, giving her a small smile before turning away and wheeling himself back to his room.

With the screaming next door finished, Graham enjoyed a final peaceful inhale of his cigarette before flicking the remains out into the open. He watched as the butt hit the tarmac of the car park, just past a collection of others. Its impact caused a celebration of embers to dance across the tarmac surface.

'A new record distance,' Graham muttered out loud again.

'Oh Graham don't make me add "Talking to himself" to your chart, we want to be removing problems not adding them!' The playful voice came from the doorway, Louise had entered Graham's room without him noticing.

Louise was also a family member of someone on the ward who had clearly had some prior experience in medicine or care. She had recently been working the ward in the absence of the doctors and nurses, making sure those left were as comfortable and looked after as best she could provide.

'I'm surprised there is room left on the chart to add anything,' Graham replied, dryly.

'They don't want many to know about this, it is a bit of a trade secret, but you can do this thing where you add additional pieces of paper to charts if more information is required, it's quite cutting edge.'

Graham let a brief smile flicker across his face. He enjoyed Louise's company, and for someone who disliked most people, that was significant. It was her bedside manner and jovial conversation that he particularly enjoyed, of late he would look forward to that more than the drugs.

'What can I help you with, Louise?'

'I have a special request actually, Graham. Lucy is concerned about people being alone when the countdown finishes and I wondered if I could bring her in here and we could all watch it together?'

Graham did not say anything. He did not want to be rude.

'That is very lovely, Louise, but I would rather be alone, and I am sure there are much nicer places you can be when...'

'Oh pish posh, Graham, I won't be having it. Everything is going to turn out fine.'

She lowered her voice into a somewhat obvious and theatrical whisper. '...But were we needed to make a sharp exit for any reason, I am probably the only person here that knows how to use the disabled lifts.' She winked and motioned to his wheelchair.

Graham grunted. He didn't want to show it, but the prospect of company was warming. Louise took that as affirmation and bounced over to him to clean his glasses, which had of late become their daily ritual.

With his glasses removed, Graham's ability to see was hampered, however, he noticed Louise was wearing a new necklace around her neck. While he was deciding whether to ask about it or not, Louise noticed him squinting.

'It's a locket, Graham,' she said happily. 'It contains a photo of my parents that my mother used to wear. I wanted them with me for the...'

Louise petered off, not quite knowing how to end that sentence.

Graham nodded in understanding.

'That is very sweet,' he added reassuringly.

As the countdown dwindled to a close and the rich ribbons of blue light ebbed to zero, Louise led Lucy in the room to watch the final few seconds. Graham nodded in acknowledgment and returned to the screen, not really knowing what to expect.

What was perhaps the last thing he was expecting, however, was for the fluid blue shapes to contort into a perfect resemblance of his face.

Graham stared at the image aghast, it was unmistakably him on the screen, albeit younger and better groomed. The shapes continued to swirl impossibly on the screen, as words below Graham's face faded slowly into recognition.

PLEASE SUBMIT GRAHAM CASTLE.

Graham snapped his head to where Louise stood across the room, hoping this to be some strange reaction to his medication or some sort of seizure. He was surprised to find that Louise and Lucy were not transfixed on the screen as he expected, but instead looking at him, concern and worry unmistakeably worn on their faces like masks.

'Is this… Who do you see on the screen, Louise? You see yourself on the screen don't you?'

Graham knew deep down that if Louise saw herself on the screen, she would not be reacting the way she currently was.

'No Graham, it's… you.'

'Mummy, what is happening??' clawed Lucy, fear now replacing the excitement that once lit up her face.

Graham wasn't sure he was aware that Lucy was Louise's daughter, and under different circumstances, he may have apologised for not connecting the dots sooner. He was understandably too distracted however to really compute this. Louise pulled Lucy close, and after a brief glance back to the television, she shuffled them both to where Graham sat, shell shocked, to place a comforting hand where his rested on the chair.

It did not take long before a hive of activity could be heard on the once desolate carpark. Graham was not really surprised that they located him so quickly, he had been at the hospital long enough for an extensive paper trail to accumulate undoubtedly.

Generic important-looking people swarmed the corridors until Graham was located and he was wheeled out, bundled into a van unceremoniously. Louise had insisted that she went with him and there was no pretending that he did not want the company now, he shared a very vulnerable and worried smile with the two girls as the van sped off towards The Visitor.

The crowd parted as the van approached ground zero, a small narrow passage emerged between the scared and confused faces from where Graham sat towards The Visitor. He saw the driver turn to face him.

'We are all here with you.'

His words were empty and meaningless, as well as a bit strange, but Graham appreciated the attempt to be supportive.

Louise helped him from the van and pointed his chair in the direction of the passage. Graham was surprised to hear a faint beeping noise coming from the Visitor, had this only just started or had he missed it amongst the news coverage?

He was distracted from his train of thought by the sound of a stifled sob behind him. As he turned, he saw Louise looking down at him with almost a heartbroken expression on her face. He patted the hand that rested on his wheelchair reassuringly.

'Don't be upset, Louise, there are worse endings to a story, I am sure,' he spoke softly. Despite the crowds around them, it seemed very quiet other than the rhythmic beeping of the Visitor. His words had done little to comfort Louise by the looks of it, tears now streaming down her face. He wanted to make a joke about the fact she was getting upset over a patient she had only known a few months, but something stopped him.

He gave her hand another squeeze, hoping that it conveyed the gratitude of not being alone in this moment that he couldn't bring himself to say.

'I didn't know Lucy was your daughter,' he said, trying to distract them both from the chaos around them. 'What a beautiful little girl you have, she will do well with you as her mother.'

'Thank you,' sniffed Louise, clutching her locket. 'I hope I can be half the role model that I had in my life.'

Graham looked around at the crowds that enveloped the van and the passageway. Stoney faced expressions looked back at him, he saw faces that he thought were familiar but, in a blink, became unrecognisable. Why was everyone so silent?

'I wish I could have known you better,' Graham said.

Louise wept openly now.

'Do you want me to push you down the passage?' she blubbered, composing herself.

All Graham could hear was the beeping of The Visitor now, probably indicating that it was time for him to make a move.

'No thank you... I would like to wheel myself if that is okay.'

Louise smiled through the tears and kissed him on his forehead. A powerful surge of emotion tore through Graham at her touch, and it took all he had not to break down. He needed to start moving before he overthought everything that was going on. He started rolling off down the passage.

Bright white light began to bubble through The Visitor's harsh metal exterior as Graham rolled through the crowds, causing him to squint. It grew and grew with an intensity he had never known, but at the same time provided the warmth of a hot shower after a cold wet day.

He was half-way there now and The Visitor almost entirely obscured by light. The beeping he heard before was becoming quieter and slower as he approached, replaced only with the warmth of the light hitting his body.

Without reason, Graham decided that he did not want to roll forward anymore. Whether it was the warmth of the light or the adrenaline pumping through his body, he thought that his legs should be able to bear the strain of this last little journey.

As Graham stood and stumbled forward like Bambi, he heard the crowd erupt around him in cheers. A joyous feeling washed over him, and he instinctively raised his hands to the sky in thanks to all those supporting him, like a rockstar to their fans. The next step forward did not come naturally, however, and Graham suddenly felt very unsure, almost scared.

The beeping was soft now, slower than before. As Graham turned to go back, he saw Louise at the bottom of the passage, Lucy in her arms. Over the commotion of the crowd, the light, the beeping, Louise's voice reached him as if she were whispering in his ear.

'We are going to be okay, Dad, you don't need to worry about us.'

Graham smiled, his body relaxing completely at Louise's words. He turned back, and with clarity and purpose, walked into the light.

CHUCK IT ON THE SCAPEGOAT

He woke to a sharp ringing in his ears and the taste of blood in his mouth. The rope holding his wrists together had started to bore into the skin, trying to adjust where they sat with the back of the chair proved a fruitless exercise.

A voice rose above the ringing.

'I'm sorry, you have been rather unfortunate, we could have picked anyone.'

The voice was unfamiliar and its source unknown.

The only trace of light was two warm yellow slivers, either side of his nose under where the blindfold sat.

The voice spoke again.

'I know you didn't choose this, but you must know that this will be for the greater good.'

'Our country is dissolving before our very eyes,' the voice continued. 'We need this to unify the people, give them a reason to band together behind parliament.'

It was only now he noticed his shoes had been removed. What felt like wooden logs could be felt underfoot.

The voice sounded closer now.

'Lying to the populace in this manner really disturbs me, it goes against... well, it all really! but if they believe it, if they believe you to be this master of evil who almost bought the country to its knees... it might save us all.'

The sound of a match being struck echoed around him as the voice continued, remorse could be sensed with each word.

'Think of it this way… you'll be immortalised in history! Much more so than sleeping rough on the streets of London was ever going to. We'll give you a name that will live on long after we all perish.'

The wooden logs began to feel warmer now, the slivers of light now dancing under the blindfold.

A door opened somewhere ahead, the voice now distant.

'The unification of the British people starts today, tomorrow's papers will sing about how we overcame the plots of terrorists, emerging from flames of imminent civil war like a phoenix, a nation bought together in anger at the attempt on our capital. The 5th of November will be remembered, I assure you of that… I just hope that God will forgive us for our sins against you, Guy.'

The door slammed shut and only the sound of crackles remained in the darkness.

The Annals of Amar

THOSE HURT IN THE DOORWAY OF CHANGE WILL BE THOSE WHO STOOD STILL

Lauren Atete

'I feel we should have probably tried harder to contact Sarah.'

'I know, darling, it doesn't sit right with me either but I went around there twice physically and called god knows how many times – there was just no answer.'

'Mmm,' acknowledged Lauren with a soft nod, fiddling with the tray latch in front of her in thought. They had been flying for about six hours now, mostly in silence. Around them, holidaymakers were revelling in the dizzying euphoria of the outbound flight, a hybrid atmosphere born of having to wake at the crack of dawn and the celebratory-alcoholic-drink-with-breakfast which for some reason became socially acceptable inside the confines of the airport.

Lauren couldn't engage with the same vibe.

'I find it strange that he requested his body be buried in Halifax, why not back home?' Lauren hoped her mother would be thinking the same, surely.

'You know your brother,' she said casually, clearly not wanting to unpick what may be a thorny question right now. She squeezed Lauren's hand briefly. 'To try and predict him would be foolhardy. Maybe he fell in love with

Canada, I've never been but I've been told it can be quite beautiful.'

'We won't have too long to see it for ourselves; in hindsight I wish we had come out for a little longer. I feel like it's going to be a rush to cram everything into three days.'

'I know, dear, but we can come back and visit when we have more time to prepare. I'm not exactly in a sightseeing mood anyway...'

It was Lauren's turn to squeeze her mum's hand. It wasn't natural for her to be so tactile. These last few days had been hard on them both.

'I'll head over to Clark's apartment first thing, if you are able to go and do the churchy elements without me, then we can meet for dinner, my treat.'

He can't have accumulated too much stuff in such a short time, thought Lauren. The landlord was going to meet her in the morning so she could pick up the keys to collect Clark's personal belongings, the rest was destined for the local charity shops.

With the conversation over, Lauren put her headphones back in and watched as the textured sky beneath transitioned out of sight. Blind Melon's 'Change' plucked into her ears and her thoughts returned to her brother.

'Did you know Stevie Nicks wrote a song about John Lennon despite never meeting him?' It was a question Clark had once asked her on the anniversary of their father's death and it was a conversation that had stuck with Lauren over the years. Their father had passed when Lauren was too young to really remember him and it would often become a point of contention and jealousy that Clark had the opportunity to get to know him where she didn't.

Lauren expected that this was a rhetorical question, and she was right.

'He is the white dove in "Edge of Seventeen",' continued

Clark. 'She wrote it after her uncle and John died in the same week.'

Wondering just how long she would need to be subjected to this intense Fleetwood-Mac-factoid phase, Lauren turned to Clark with the full angst of a moody teenager.

'Great, and how exactly is that relevant?'

'Because they had never met, and she created something beautiful despite never having that connection. I mention it because… just because you didn't have much time with Dad doesn't mean he won't impact your life in a similar way. Maybe he will inspire your "Edge of Seventeen".'

While Lauren dismissed this at the time, the sentiment remained. Would she have pursued a career in teaching had her father not been a lecturer? It was hard to say, but she often wondered if it was her homage to him.

With Clark's passing, Lauren reflected how she would go about processing his death. Unlike with their father, Lauren and Clark had been extremely close and so this approach to grief felt new and unfamiliar.

How can I ensure Clark continues to play a key role in my life going forward? she asked herself, *what will his white dove be to me?*

This level of introspection proved far too much of a burden for this time of the morning. Putting these questions to the side for now, Lauren leaned back into the chair and let the twangy southern sounds of Blind Melon clear her mind, letting her worries drift by as the clouds were below.

Lauren Atete

Clark's apartment was a state.

Had she have known how much of a slob her brother had regressed into here in Halifax she may have just said to the landlord to bin the whole lot. Disgusted but determined, she opened her sixth bin liner and continued to slide various plates and mugs from the kitchen top into it indiscriminately.

Despite the mess, the day had been relatively therapeutic and had given Lauren a chance to feel close to her brother again. She had been selecting songs that they had both enjoyed, filling the silence as she shuffled through the trinket-laden space. Currently 'Man in the Mirror' by Michael Jackson bounced around the small apartment and Lauren was ashamed to catch herself swaying absent-mindedly to the beat as she would on a much happier occasion.

About two hours into the search for Clark's important documents, Lauren stumbled across a couple of concerning items which caused her to pause. Tucked haphazardly behind a bundle of old jeans appeared to be some evidence of her brother's relationship with drugs. A small bottle labelled *morphine* sat beside a similar sized but unidentifiable vessel, just the words *for emergencies* scribbled on its surface.

Lauren was no stranger to the world of drugs and had it not been for her career would have likely still dabbled in the softer world of the Devil's Lettuce to this day. Bottles of morphine and this other unknown substance were far outside her comfort zone however and questions of how well she really knew her brother bubbled up uncomfortably in her head.

What made this discovery even more peculiar was the addition of a small, folded piece of paper stuffed under the vials. Lauren carefully unravelled it to reveal just a small sentence.

If found, please play 'I Just Want To Sell Out My Funeral' by the Wonder Years as my funeral song.

Lauren studied the single line closely, confirming it was definitely Clark's handwriting, feeling utterly perplexed. There was no denying that the final song of their 'The

Greatest Generation' album was a masterpiece, but was it suitable as a funeral song? Despite the subject matter, *which was a bit on the nose*, it didn't really give the traditional vibe you would associate with a parting song, and to Lauren's recollection, it wasn't really a genre of music that Clark had shown any affinity towards before either.

People change I guess, she concluded, slightly disgruntled, annoyed with herself for getting upset that Clark dared to evolve as a person.

I would have thought he would want a Scorpions track as his funeral song, Winds of Change or something...

The shrill of an unfamiliar doorbell chime ripped Lauren's attention away. Looking down the hall in mild alarm, she saw the silhouette of a uniformed individual looming through the distorted glass.

Cautiously, and with care not to trip over the discarded bags of Clark's belongings, Lauren approached the door pocketing the vials and small note. Ensuring the chain was on, she eased the door open tentatively. The figure outside appeared to be a Canadian police officer although Lauren did feel momentarily disappointed that the red overcoat and Mountie hat apparel, she had associated with Canadian law enforcement, wasn't an accurate representation. This officer wore the standard shades of blue and black seen across the anglosphere, with a badge that read *Sergeant Glen Thomas* pinned to his breast.

'Good morning, Miss, are you a relative of the deceased?' Lauren was surprised to hear he didn't have a thick accent and welcomed the feeling of familiarity found within Sergeant Thomas' voice.

'Uh, hello, yes, I am his sister, Clark's sister I mean.' The thought to correct herself and say 'was' bubbled inside her, but Lauren squashed the idea down with instant resentment – she was not ready for that transition just yet.

Slightly more confident that this person wasn't a serial axe murderer, Lauren unchained the door and opened it wider.

'Fantastic,' responded Sergeant Thomas, clasping his hands together with a single clap. 'I was hoping someone would be in.'

Lauren smiled silently, standing patiently waiting for further context to this visit. She was very aware of the drug paraphernalia in her pocket. *Do Canadian police search random people?* Surely not, thought Lauren, but she did not want to risk letting him inside just in case.

Sergeant Thomas appeared to notice the pause, as well as the lack of an invitation inside.

'I'll keep this brief as I am sure you have a lot on your plate at the moment, Miss. I am not sure if you are aware or not, but the search team earlier identified a couple of unidentifiable liquids in your brother's residence which we wanted to seize for testing. Unfortunately, at the time, they didn't have the evidence bags available but I'm here now with some fresh ones.'

Sergeant Thomas waved a pair of translucent bags up playfully, either pretending not to acknowledge the sensitivity of the conversation or just breezing over it. 'I don't know if you have come across these liquids at all have you? I have been told they are in clear vials.'

Lauren repeated the paused smile and flicked her eyes up in feigned recollection to buy some thinking time. What was going on here? It seemed peculiar. She wasn't sure if police officers would just leave potential drugs on a premises after searching it, however she admittedly was not an expert in this field. *Damn, I wish Sarah was here*, she thought, continuing the smile and charade.

'Ummm, no, I don't think so, Officer, no, sorry.'

Besides, how suspicious would it look to produce them from my pocket now?

Sergeant Thomas' posture and expression didn't change, but his tone did. This was not the answer he had expected to receive.

'I would kindly ask you think carefully if you have, Miss, it is important we recover those liquids.'

The change in temperament made Sergeant Thomas appear more familiar to Lauren than before, perhaps it was the sudden authoritarian disapproval she recognised from her days getting caught smoking weed in the park.

Maybe.

Why hadn't the officer just entered the apartment though? Surely, he would be in possession of the same warrant this previous search team had.

There were too many strange questions here for a day that was already emotionally taxing as it was and Lauren certainly did not want to incriminate the memory of her late brother by passing over evidence of whatever demons he was plagued by.

'I appreciate that, Sergeant…'

Maybe calling him 'Officer' wasn't helping, let's try respecting the rank to diffuse the situation.

'…but I am only here to pick up a few of my brother's personal effects and have not really dived too deep into the apartment at this stage,' she lied, hoping the black sacks around her feet would go unnoticed. 'I'll be done shortly if you would like to come back later?'

A thin but unmistakably disappointed smile flashed upon the sergeant's face. Lauren wasn't initially sure if that would conclude their conversation or not, however the buoyant and playful character from earlier returned with an agreeable and enthusiastic nod.

'Of course, of course, Miss. As I say, I appreciate you have a lot going on right now. I will return much later; you please take your time now.'

With a tip of his hat, Sergeant Thomas smiled again and turned to leave. As she watched him walk away, Lauren was careful to notice his gait alter significantly once he thought he was out of her line of sight.

What a bizarre encounter.

Lauren returned to the apartment and thumbed the incriminating vials in her pocket in thought. Had she done the right thing? She had no intention of holding onto them for long, but if removing them from this apartment would prevent blemishing her brother's good name... it was worth it.

Lauren Atete

Clark's funeral drew a larger crowd than expected, especially considering they were half the world away from their immediate family and friends. Lauren was heartened to see Clark had made so many connections in his short time in Halifax, presumably from Erogen.

The minister spoke through the usual eulogy, peppered with personal stories supplied by Lauren and her mother. A part of her regretted bringing these memories of her brother to this environment, as if the occasion would now corrupt them and leave them forever bittersweet to think back on.

They were not for her now though, Lauren reflected, as these stories were for those who didn't have the privilege of knowing her brother, to understand the life he led before they knew him.

Her eyes didn't leave the casket in front of them as the minister rambled on. She had her own thoughts of what she wanted to say to Clark and did so only in her head, willing the internal conversation she was having to travel through the wood before her and into the body she knew that laid inside. After some time, a tightening of her mother's hand told her that they were nearing the end of the service.

Not to go against what appeared to be her brother's final wish, Lauren had informed the organisers to play the song he requested from The Wonder Years. There were bound to be some confused glances as the coffin was lowered to the sound of angsty pop punk, but Lauren thought that actually this could be very on-brand for her brother. Clark was always one to keep people on their toes.

As her brother was lowered into the ground, Lauren finally braved the sight and faces of those who had come to grieve and say their final goodbyes.

Ashen expressions stood all around her.

Contrasting the respectful silence around them, the thrashing of drums and Dan Campbell's screaming vocals demanded Lauren's attention more and she chose to slip into her own thoughts once again.

A nudge from her mother bought her out of the music and back to the moment, followed by a subtle nod to the crowd in front of them. Navigating the grief, Lauren identified what her mother was motioning towards standing quietly behind a group of miscellaneous 30-somethings.

Sarah was here.

The Wonder Years continued to wash over Lauren like a lapping tide as she studied her Sister-in-law incredulously. Sarah had aged since they last met, but gracefully. She stood stoic at the back of the crowd and while this was likely intentional to pay respects from a distance and not draw attention, Lauren wanted to bring her to them. They were family after all.

Like her, Sarah appeared to be watching the others rather than the body of her ex-husband being lowered into the ground. Noticeably, Sarah appeared to be looking intently at an area half-way between the two of them amongst the circular crowd.

Lauren followed her eyes. Her gaze fell upon a well-dressed man in what appeared to be his early to mid-40s, round black sunglasses obscured his eyes leaving just his shaven head and grey-flecked beard as prominent features to analyse.

This man must be important, considered Lauren, noting the two obvious security guards who sat either side of him. *Who brings security guards to a funeral?*

A shuffle of bodies behind the guards caught Lauren's attention and as she focused behind them, a sharp chill ran down the middle of her back. Sergeant Thomas was stood just behind the three men, looming once again like he had on the entrance to Clark's apartment. He was not wearing a uniform now however, and with his face and head no longer obscured by a policeman's hat Lauren could see a mop of dark black hair. Suddenly the familiarity she had felt earlier hit like a freight train as she stared into a face she now recognised as the criminal Hasira Fansa.

Words immediately escaped her, and she clutched at her mother's hand tightly in panic. Before she could alert her, or elaborate any further, the bald man Sarah was watching appeared to become quite agitated, turning to leave.

Lauren watched as Hasira stepped forward to place a preventative hand upon his shoulder, preventing his exit. He looked up to Hasira, startled and confused.

The man's jaw dropped, presumably both in shock and to attract the attention of the guards to his side. Lauren couldn't tell if he managed to make a sound due to the thrashing music surrounding them, Hasira had reacted swiftly however and lifted what appeared to be a small firearm from his jacket and placed the barrel inside the man's aghast mouth.

He smirked, holding the back of the man's neck with his

free hand as he tried to flail away, forcing their eyes to meet. The man gagged on the weapon and frantically slapped the bodies around him for aid.

Hasira appeared to whisper something in the man's ear while the now alerted guards snatched at the grip on their employer, one trying to pull Hasira's arm down with his body weight.

It remained firm.

The song was beginning to fade out now, and the silence it left coincided with the sudden jarring explosion of a gunshot that ripped through the distracted crowd. Heads ducked and snapped to the source as shrieks erupted from the mourners closer to the chaos, Lauren threw a protective arm over her mother, watching in horror as the man's body staggered backwards, falling and hitting the ground just shy of the grave where Clark's own body now rested.

Eight Years Later

'Amari, your hand was up first I think?'

'2026.'

'Well done, and who were the first three nations to sign the treaty? – Ebex – you.'

'America, Russia and… Germany?'

'Close, Ebex, Belgium, not Germany.'

Lauren smiled warmly at the class before her, the energy had been high in the classroom today and they had managed to get through a lot.

She loved these days.

'Okay, class, if you could all turn to the chapter on New World Collaboration within The Amarism, have a read and answer the questions in the quiz app on the same section, thank you.'

In time gone by the room would have erupted with the sound of pages being ruffled through and pencils scratching on paper to this request. Time had changed in the education world, however.

'Miss Atete, my advert has frozen and I can't open the material,' whined Seb, looking around with frustration at everyone else who was busily swiping through the pages.

'Are your earphones connected properly to the tablet? The advert won't let you progress to the text unless it knows you are actually listening to it, Seb.'

A finger to his ear and a resigned sigh from Seb's desk told Lauren that the issue was likely now resolved. She turned to her desk to conduct some long overdue admin.

Amongst the faculty communications and usual parental queries was a bright red 'Government Bulletin' email sitting atop the inbox, a small clock icon sat adjacent to it. Lauren was thankful the clock remained green, the last government bulletin that she hadn't read in time had earned her a disciplinary.

Pairing her own earphones, she opened the bulletin and reclined in the chair to listen to the video.

BREAKING NEWS: The Press Secretary can confirm that the terrorist Sarah Atete has been captured in an organised raid this morning north of Vancouver, near Whistler. No injuries have been reported and Ms Atete is currently being transported to a secure facility for processing and trial. The Minister of Foreign Affairs and Acting Science Secretary Gordon Huringa had this to say...

Lauren rolled her eyes briefly.

Gordon Huringa needed no introduction, she retorted to herself, exasperated. She had become increasingly tired of seeing Gordon's over-manufactured face on most of the recent government bulletins, particularly around those involving The Resistance. She wasn't sure why someone needed that much plastic surgery to love themselves in this day and age but that was neither here nor there.

The bulletin continued.

'… *I think this morning's operation brings a very satisfying end to what was an extremely distressing and damaging period of our lives for everyone. No longer will our communities have to fear the radicalised barbarians that threatened our way of life. I promise to you as a member of parliament, and as a member of our society, that justice will be swift, and representative of the damage Atete and her campaign of destruction has caused.'*

'Yesterday has now gone,' He concluded, nodding encouragingly to a presumed crowd of reporters hanging off his every word. *'It has gone and it's time to think of tomorrow. A new chapter. Don't stop thinking of it, don't take it out of your mind, for it is here now, and it will be better than before, I promise you.'*

Lauren had zoned out already, thinking intently. With a cursory look over the distracted pupils in front of her, she reached into her desk drawer. Clicking and releasing a false wall at the back, she carefully cradled the contents that lay behind before they tumbled into the main body of the drawer.

In her hand now was a selection of notes, a vial and, crucially, an old mobile phone. Careful not to touch the handset with her fingerprints, Lauren used the notes to pivot the screen into view. Even with the brightness down low, she could see an unread message adorned atop the display.

Phase 2 a go – proceed as planned – HF

She left the message 'unread', returning the items behind the false wall and sliding a small latch to keep it in place. Plausible deniability was key here, the hidden phone would be suspicious enough without a deleted message found through the inevitable forensic examination. Pretending she had no knowledge of the hidden section would be easier, particularly with the scrap notes framing another teacher within the school. Devilish, yes, but necessary.

Lauren disconnected her earphones and reflected on the day. Somewhere down the hall someone was practising piano.

Sarah had been caught. It was only a matter of time really. The last of The Resistance strongholds had fallen earlier this week, as she discovered through the Gordon-led government bulletins demanding attention within her inbox.

The student down the hall had started playing the piano properly now and Sarah recognised the melody as John Lennon's 'Imagine'. She listened casually, once again reviewing the class in front of her. She wondered what world awaited them over the next few months and, more selfishly, what the history books would say of her involvement in what was to come.

SIX PICK UP STICKS

The wild camping was a bust and the boys were trudging back in the rain.

'…I mean, on the plus side, at least we are going to be sleeping in comfy beds tonight now,' chipped Adam.

A symphony of reluctant agreement followed. The intention had been to celebrate their 30th birthdays with a night in the woods like they had done in times gone by, this time with an added sense of adventure and risk that came with doing the whole thing without a tent.

Despite a keen eye on the weather that day, the predictions had betrayed the event and, notwithstanding the best attempts to see the rain out, there was no chance of an enjoyable night's sleep on the cold wet detritus.

Spirits were understandably low, not only because of the change of plans but because they had travelled 40 minutes deep into the woods to avoid detection. This was now an uncomfortable and wet 40 minutes back to the car.

'Thank god you put that marker on the car, Alex,' Adam said again, his positivity not yet infecting the rest of the group. 'We would have had no hope getting back otherwise.'

'This is true,' agreed Marvin, probably the most embittered by the retreat home. 'I lost my bearings the moment we deviated off the bridleway.'

'I think it would have been fine had it still been light out,' Ollie contributed, the torch on his phone leading the group through the thicket. 'But I agree, I feel much better for Alex using Maps. Takes the pressure off!'

'I was quite surprised by the level of signal we got out here, actually,' Alex added, checking the app to make sure they were going in the right direction.

'I know, Fred was even able to stream that playlist!' exclaimed Ben, who was finding the camping chairs cumbersome to carry back. '...Kind of ruined my plans to creep us all out with ghost stories and signal-less phones tonight.'

Ollie chuckled. 'Ha, and the fact that Marvin brought like six power banks. No chance of us running out of battery.'

'...Could have powered half of Didcot with all your kit, Marvin,' Adam joked.

'I only brought two,' replied Marvin, defensively. His prepared packing for the trip had already been the butt of several jokes this evening. 'One for the phones and another for the speakers if we needed it, hardly overkill!'

'Right, right right,' Ollie added, smiling.

The group had navigated themselves through the first wood which had originally been their destination for the night and were now skirting a large corn field that they had walked past earlier that day.

Marvin sighed longingly at the crops. 'I was looking forward to a corn on the cob buffet in the morning.'

'How do you know they are ripe? I've never picked corn before,' said Ben.

'Hmm, it says here to look for the ones with brown string-like fur on,' Alex added, his face illuminated by his phone.

'Very appealing,' joked Fred, 'are you sure you didn't accidentally google a Kiwi, Alex?'

A light chuckle ran through the group.

'How far away are we now, Alex?' Fred asked, stretching his neck in discomfort as he hauled back all the beers they had expected to drink.

'Not too far actually now, it says we are only about three to four minutes away from where I placed the marker, hmm....'

'Hmmm? What's up?' pressed Ollie, turning his torch around to illuminate Alex.

'No, nothing, it's just, this walk felt a lot longer earlier. I'm pretty sure we'd been walking a while before getting to the corn field.'

'Now you mention it yeah, we can't be just a couple of minutes away,' said Ben, concerned.

Adam looked around from where they had emerged from the wood and reviewed the surrounding area.

'Well we might not have gone the most efficient route to the woods earlier, perhaps we doubled back on ourselves a bit without realising?'

The group murmured variations of 'good point' and 'that's probably it', all satisfied with Adam's explanation.

It soon became apparent, as the route returned them deeper into the woods from which they came, that something was not quite right with the app. Emerging from thicket on the other side, the boys found themselves on a previously unseen and well-maintained stretch of land.

Alex restarted his phone, frustrated.

'...I'm not sure what's gone on here,' he added, looking around.

'What's that up there?' asked Marvin, motioning down the channel of land between the woods, to what appeared to be a large manor at the grounds' end.

Ollie span, trying to get his bearings.

'I can't be certain...' he said slowly, as if the surrounding trees would somehow provide the answers. '…but we might have wandered onto the National Trust property that was adjacent to our camp spot.'

The group squinted down at the manor. It was a beautiful building, extravagant architecture in mottled stone, small squares of rich amber shone from the many windows facing them.

It was presently occupied.

'You are not going to believe this…' Alex was still frantically pinching and swiping at his phone. The boys all turned to him apprehensively. 'But the marker is now placed right above that building.'

'Bullshit,' declared Ollie, stomping over to look at Alex's phone. 'It can't be.'

'Nope,' said Fred bluntly, shaking his head in dismissal of Alex's statement. 'Say something else, Alex please, I'm not accepting that.'

'Have you tried refreshing it?' piped Ben, unhelpfully.

'Yes.'

'What about if you close the app down and re-open it?' offered Marvin.

'Yes, twice, it's still showing up at the building regardless.'

'Can you share the link with me please? Maybe on my phone it'll say something different.' Adam withdrew his own phone and awaited the vibration to alert him that Alex had sent through the link.

Everyone's phone vibrated. The faces of the boys were all illuminated against the pressing dark as they each eagerly reviewed the link Alex had sent. Mild panic began to reflect in their eyes, each pinching and swiping at the screen for their own answers.

Ollie looked around the group, deciding to break the silence.

'Guys, it's fine. A bit weird but it's fine. Look, someone is clearly in and awake in that house. Let's just go in and ask for directions to a car park – or at least the nearest road – we'll be able to find our way back then surely.'

'Absolutely not,' Fred retorted again. '…Stuff of nightmares that, Ollie, have you lost your mind?'

'Yeah, Ollie mate, I'm not sure we need to do that…' Marvin said cautiously, clearly searching for a reason not to approach the manor other than that he was spooked out by the idea.

Adam put his phone back in his pocket and flicked the rain from his eyes, looking at the manor again.

'I'm not convinced we need to be worried about asking them for directions, lads. The application does say this is a National Trust place, it's not like it's some haunted house that doesn't exist on the map. I say we go and knock.'

Ben nodded his head in agreement. 'Yeah, c'mon, we're getting soaked here, let's not drag this night out.'

'Fred, if you're dead set at not going why don't you stay here with the gear to save us lugging it up to the house and back?' Ollie cocked a small smile as he spoke, challenging Fred.

Fred blew the collecting rainwater off his moustache.

'Fuck off, Ollie. Just a string of bad ideas from you today.'

Noticing the rising tensions, Alex also returned his phone to his pocket and put his hands up in defeat.

'Okay, okay, we are just standing in the rain now. Ollie, you may have a point about not carrying all the stuff further than we need to. Why don't three of us stay with the kit and the other three go to the manor and ask for some assistance or something?'

'Sounds good to me,' agreed Ben. 'I'm happy to head to the house.'

'Me too,' volunteered Adam, 'I presume you're also coming, Ollie?'

'Yep,' Ollie said, dropping his bags with relief. 'I needed a break from lugging all this about anyway. Are you three all okay to wait here?'

Fred and Alex both nodded and looked to Marvin, who had remained in thought throughout this exchange.

'Marvin?' Adam pressed. 'You can come with us if you want.'

'No no. I'll stay here with Fred and Alex,' he said decidedly. 'I mean this whole thing has a *split up and search for clues* vibe but I guess three and three is the safest split.' He dropped the camping stool he was carrying on his back with sudden enthusiasm. 'Plus, we get to stay with the beer, so it's a win/win as far as I'm concerned.'

Ollie, Adam and Ben set off down the grounds towards the manor, following the linear path of lawn lined by thick woodland growth. No longer encumbered by the camping gear, the walk would almost have been pleasant if not for the weather.

After some time, Ben looked back at the party they had left behind, just making out the shapes of Marvin, Fred and Alex huddled together under the shelter of a nearby tree, camping chairs assembled and beers in hand.

'They're alright I think,' he said aloud, unsure if it was the other two, or himself, he was reassuring.

With the manor closer upon them, it became apparent shapes were moving in front of the windows and the soft hum of music bled into the darkness towards them.

'Looks like some sort of party is going on,' said Ollie enthusiastically.

Adam nodded. 'Makes this whole approach less creepy I guess.'

'Yeah, fuck a soggy beer, we might get some champagne out of this!' Ollie slapped Adam and Ben on the back with zest, looking over his shoulder back to the three they had left behind and laughing.

Ben didn't quite share the passion for the situation.

'Wait, you're not planning on going inside, are you, Ollie? I thought we were just asking for directions, maybe a taxi but directions at least, then bolting?' he pressed, looking between both Adam and Ollie as they stepped up to the manor's porch.

The music was louder now, strings and piano keys could be heard beyond the grey stone barrier. Figures could be seen dancing behind the veiled windows with a spritely energy and flair, pairs of people entangled to the rhythm of whatever band was playing therein.

'…Well, I mean, Ben…' Adam bounced his head to the sides, feigning internal conflict on the topic. 'If they invite us in, they invite us in. By the looks of some of the frocks and dinner suits inside we may just score some caviar in addition to some bubbly!'

'Haha! That's it, boy!' Ollie clapped Adam on the back again. 'C'mon , we'll be in and out in no time. I'll text the others now that there's some sort of party going on so there will likely be taxis coming.' He squinted up at the manor, blinking at the raindrops, counting the windows.

'Yeah, there are bound to be taxis coming for this lot,' he concluded, noting the difference between apparent dancers and number of rooms. 'At the very least, let's explain our situation and then go around and wait in their drive for the first available taxi.'

Ollie pulled out his phone and tapped away, crafting a quick message. Ben felt his pocket vibrate, presumably from Ollie messaging the group chat. Without checking his own phone, Ben turned to look back at Alex, Marvin and Fred again. Against the battering rain he thought he could just make out the illumination of a phone, possibly two.

Pretending he was satisfied, and not at all reluctant, Ben nodded to Ollie who smiled broadly.

Taking the initiative, Adam picked up the doorknocker and tapped it against the old wooden door with three confident hits.

The patter of heavy rain pressing against them suddenly became all they could hear, as the music and thunder of dancing inside instantly died.

The sudden reaction from inside welcomed an uneasy glance between the boys, each showing a mixture of bemusement and apprehension. Shadows no longer circled behind the window's veil and above, Ben thought he saw the twitch of a far curtain from one of the manor's many floors.

After what seemed an inappropriate amount of time to answer the door, the careful thumbing of several locks could be heard from behind the dark ornate wood.

Eventually, and with clear caution, the door eased open ever so slightly, partially revealing the face of a man inside. Bewildered at the theatrics of the situation, Ollie stepped forward.

'Good evening, sir, I'm sorry to bother you, but my friends and I were trekking in the woods and have gotten turned around. I was wondering…'

A gruff and inaudible whisper from the man behind the door interrupted Ollie.

'Sorry, I didn't quite catch that, what did you say?'

'I asked,' the whisper came again, this time with increased volume and irritability. 'Are you alone?'

'Well.' Ollie paused, unsure as to whether there was a need to explain the full three and three split of the group at this point. 'It's just us three right now yes, but a few of our other friends are back up the grounds with our bags. You can see their light I think.'

The man shot a quick look up towards where Ollie

indicated, although his focus appeared to be more on the woods around them rather than the boys themselves.

He began muttering to himself again '…Too many distractions probably, quickly now.'

Catching the boys off guard, the door was flung open with vigour. As the man ushered them inside, they each cast a look behind for the urgency they had apparently missed.

Once inside the threshold of the manor, they were met with a congregation of intense expressions. The ground level was heaving with people, more than initially seemed logical compared to the quiet and isolated nature of the manor itself. A frozen atmosphere had apparently gripped the revellers from the boys' intrusion, with even the dancers remaining on the spot where the music stopped to assess the newcomers.

It was not only the cold reception of the people that was unnerving, but the vibe of the whole party. The women all wore polonaise and Victorian evening dresses, with the men in dinner suits and tails. The interior was as majestic as the outside suggested, monochrome stone now replaced with rich red and mustard yellows with flamboyant curtains draped from the ceiling.

The boys smiled to the onlookers nervously, when the man who had welcomed them suddenly spoke loudly to their audience.

'It is fine ladies and gentlemen, it is just these three, let the festivities continue!'

Ben noticed his voice no longer carried the gruffness and concern it did at the door, but could not linger on the thought long before the commanded revelry around them erupted once more.

Music, dance and laughter continued as if the arrival of the boys had not occurred at all. Men and women flung themselves around to the music of an unseen band and several butlers continued their rotations, carrying trays of Champagne flutes and canapés to the guests.

Ben, Ollie and Adam stood awkwardly in the entrance, watching the performance before them as if put on for just their benefit. The joy was infectious and for a moment Ben forgot about little else other than the desire to fling himself around to the music.

The man who had welcomed them into the manor remained next to them, eyeing the crowd and nodding gently in satisfaction, a foot tapping to the beat carelessly. After the boys had been given enough time to take in the atmosphere, he spoke.

'Well, what can I do you for you, boys?' he asked, pleasantly.

Ollie tore his eyes from the dancing and faced the gentleman. He was an older man, maybe in his 60s. His beard thin like the hair on his head.

'We just need to call a taxi, if that is not too much trouble, we must have taken a wrong turn or something on our hike earlier and can't find our way back to the car.'

The man smiled warmly at the request. Ben noticed his eyes didn't quite reflect the sentiment.

'Of course, of course,' he said nodding. 'Do you need to use the telephone?'

'No no, we have phones thank you, we just need to know where... this is? Where do we direct the taxi to?' Adam looked around the room as he spoke, as if to ascertain the location from the décor alone.

The man nodded. 'I understand. Please, come to the foyer out the back with me. The drive and approaching road are visible from there, I'll call you a lift.'

Ollie returned the man's smile politely. 'Thank you, that's fantastic, I'm happy to call the taxi, however, it's no bother.' He took out his phone as he spoke. 'We have been a burden enough tonight!'

The man looked from Ollie to the phone in his hand and back again, pausing for moment looking slightly confused, as if Ollie had just brandished an octopus from his pocket instead. He quickly recovered himself.

'I'll call you a lift, you have been no burden at all, please, if you will follow me.'

The peculiarity of the exchange was only exacerbated further by several of the guests closest to them also pausing to suddenly observe the conversation.

Ben smiled shyly to them, pretending not to feel uncomfortable, and turned to address Ollie and Adam.

'Listen, you boys go out the back with…' Ben gestured to the man next to them, hoping for an introduction to make further conversations a little less weird.

When none came, Ben continued, 'Our host…? I'll give the other boys a call to come on down and we can all wait for a lift in the dry together. Providing that it's okay for all of us to wait in the foyer?'

'An inspired idea,' the Host said enthusiastically, displaying again a questionably authentic smile. 'Come, you will wait just through here.'

The Host motioned for Ollie and Adam to proceed through a door near them, as they passed him, the Host turned to Ben. 'I would ask that you wait for me to open the door to your guests please.'

Ben watched Ollie and Adam follow the man, the three of them shooting mildly uncertain expressions at each other. Once out of sight, Ben pulled out his phone and dialled Fred.

The call rang out. There was no answer.

Frustrated, Ben called Marvin.

The call rang out, again there was no answer.

Ben peeked through the doorway window. The pattern on the glass obscured most of what lay beyond, several small flecks of light that could be the three other boys were still apparent against the shifting blackness of swaying trees however.

With a reassuring look behind him that he was in fact in a room full of other adults, and therefore presumably the increasing panic he was feeling was unfounded, Ben dialled Alex's phone.

As the call rang, he looked down at the door's many locks that they had heard the Host manoeuvre to allow them in. Ben didn't really like the idea of being trapped in this weird renaissance disco, and so with a final look back to make sure no one was watching, he quietly pulled the bolts back on all five of them.

The call continued to ring out, but just before Ben hung up, it connected.

'Alex! Thank God, hey, this place is a decent, if somewhat strange, shelter. Why don't you and the other two head down and wait for a taxi with us? Ollie and Adam are calling one now.'

Silence returned.

'Alex? Did you get that? If you can hear me, head on down to the manor.'

A soft, playful, giggle could be heard on the other end. Ben plugged his other ear to hear better.

'Alex! Boys! Don't fuck around now please, can you hear me?'

The band concluded their current song and the lull between allowed Ben to pick up the sound of slow breathing at the other end of the line. He checked his phone screen.

Calling ALEX 00:52…00:53…

It was certainly Alex's phone he was connected to; Ben shrank a little and returned his to his ear.

'Boys?'

The giggle returned, this time louder. It was high pitched

and somewhat manic. As the giggle subsided, a female voice spoke.

'*One, Two, Buckle my shoe,*' they sang, lazily.

Ben wasn't aware goosebumps could pierce so fiercely, as the sound of the nursery rhyme caused his whole body to react in prickly terror.

'*Three, Four, Knock at the door,*' continued the lullaby.

Turning away from the shifting shadows of the window, Ben looked to address the other guests. Hoping someone could make sense of this.

'*Five, Six, Pick Up Sticks.*'

'Alex, Fred or Marvin if you can hear me at all please come to the manor now, if this is a joke, you've got me good, but let's cut it out,' urged Ben, continuing to hold the phone to his ear as he strode into the dancing crowd.

'*Seven, Eight, Lay them straight.*'

As he immersed himself amongst the dancing, it was becoming clear none of the guests were interested in making eye contact with him. In fact, many were actively avoiding him, spinning, and spiralling away as he approached.

'*Eleven, Twelve, Dig and Delve.*'

'EXCUSE ME!' Ben shouted to the room. 'Excuse me! I would like to talk to someone in charge please?'

The dancers did not react to Ben's shout, continuing to spin shapes around the room as the music swelled.

Ben made to walk towards the source of the music. If they can pause a song at the drop of a hat when there are a couple of knocks at the door, then they can pause the song for an emergency.

Was it an emergency though? Ben questioned himself briefly. This was all getting a bit out of hand and surreal. Maybe he was overreacting.

'*Thirteen, Fourteen, Maids a-courting,*' sang the voice down the phone.

Nope, concluded Ben. *I consider this an emergency.*

As he stepped towards the back of the room, the band's location and the individual musicians became clear.

Ben's gut lurched.

Standing to the side, placidly hitting a pair of tambourines to the beat, Ollie and Adam stood with immaculate posture in full dinner suits. They faced the revellers as they tapped their tambourines, broad and encouraging smiles upon both of their faces.

Ben ran to them.

'What. *The fuck...?*' Ben whispered to them, catching their attention.

Ollie and Adam turned to face him. Happy but confused expressions filled their smiling faces, as if they did not recognise him.

'Fifteen, Sixteen, Maids in the Kitchen,' continued in his ear.

'Boys, boys, let's get out of here!' he said, pulling at their arms.

They would not budge, shaking Ben off and returning to watch their audience.

After being actively avoided by the dancers, an approaching figure to Ben's left caught his attention. The Host came forth from the crowd, eyes wide and glistening in Ben's direction.

'Please, my boy, let them play.'

Ben stumbled back away from him, raising an arm to express the desire for distance. The man appeared to ignore this, continuing to advance. He spoke to Ben directly again.

'I would ask if you would kindly hang up your telephone and come with me to the foyer, your lift is here!'

'Seventeen eighteen, Maids in waiting,' trickled through the phone as Ben lowered it from his ear and into his pocket, contemplating his options.

He looked to Ollie and Adam, who paid Ben no attention at all despite being right next to him.

'I'll come back for you,' he whispered, pivoting and darting for the door they arrived through.

'NO DON'T,' screamed the Host to his left, Ben felt the clutch of his hand against his jacket, shrugging it off before the Host could fully grip it. Ben hadn't noticed that his coat had been dripping water through the house, neither had the Host as he stepped and slipped on the puddle where Ben previously stood.

As Ben reached the door, the music predictably stopped. He took one last look behind as he flung it open, assessing if anyone else was going to try and grab him.

Everyone, from the dancers to the Host upon the floor, was still, each looking past Ben with the utmost horror.

The air stood still, and Ben followed everyone's eyes beyond him to the open door.

'Nineteen, Twenty, My plate's empty,' giggled a woman in front of Ben, who he recognised as the voice on the phone. She was old and frail, wearing a traditional housekeeping uniform.

The woman curtseyed Ben briefly with surprising agility, before stepping into the room, her black dress and white apron flicking past him.

Shrieks and screams exploded at the presence of the woman, who giggled joyfully at the reaction.

Ben couldn't see her full face from behind, but as the giggles subsided, he saw quick and unnatural movements spasming in her jaw. It was only when the woman turned to face the Host on the floor that Ben could see she now possessed a mouth far too large for her face, as if the corners of her mouth had been dragged back behind her neck.

She bore long and thin elongated teeth, rows and rows of them similar to a whale's baleen.

Frozen in shock, Ben couldn't move. He watched helplessly as the woman pounced like a predator, landing on top of the Host, howling into the room with a shrill scream before sinking her teeth deep into the Host's neck, a mist of red jetting out against the mustard yellow drapes beside them.

The room was mayhem and with some conviction Ben managed to tear his eyes from the feasting woman towards the band where Ollie and Adam had stood.

The tambourines they joyfully beat just moments before span discarded on the floor.

They've escaped, Ben hoped, turning to the open door. He focused on the specks of light where they had left Alex, Fred and Marvin.

Without looking behind, he ran back into the night.

'...Nah, I'm fucking drenched, I hate this. My tinny is more rainwater than beer at this point.'

'Quit bitching, Fred, you could have it worse. Poor Alex's wet look gel is probably running into his eyes!'

'Hey!'

'Haha! That's fair, I'm annoyed that you don't let anyone else use your time machine, Alex. I think shops stopped selling wet look in the '90s you fucking dinosaur!'

'Ah fuck you, Fred,' Alex spat, smiling despite the insult, while throwing what remained of his beer in Fred's direction.

Marvin roared with laughter between them, leaning back to avoid the crossfire.

'I wouldn't expect someone with no more than four hair follicles...' started Alex before breaking off, distracted by something behind the two of them.

Fred and Marvin followed his eyes and looked behind. A figure was quickly progressing towards them from the manor.

'Is that one of the boys?' Alex asked, squinting through the rainfall.

'It is!' proclaimed Fred. 'Ha, it's Ben absolutely booking it!'

Marvin laughed, cheering him.

'Looks like the trip to the manor didn't go very well,' he joked. '...Fucking, Dame Jessica Ennes over there, look at him!'

Alex howled with laughter.

'Why Jessica Ennes?!' he asked incredulously. 'Could you not think of any male runners?'

'Of course I can,' Marvin responded flatly, as if that resolved the matter. A pause pressed the issue, however. 'There's uhh... Linford Lightfoot.'

It was Fred's turn to laugh into the night, holding his stomach.

'Linford Lightfoot?? Do you not mean Linford Christie?'

'Yeah.' Marvin nodded. 'He likes his mates to call him Linny Lightfoot though.'

Though the laughter continued, the boys watched Ben closely; as he approached, a sense of concern bubbled among them.

Alex was the first to address it.

'Maybe we should start packing up the gear? If Ben's running, we might need to make a quick getaway.'

'Mmm,' pondered Fred, now also squinting. He could make out Ben's face and his expression worried him. 'I don't know though, we should probably wait for Adam and Ollie before moving off, they must be close behind.'

No other shapes could be seen following.

'Maybe they're going through the trees?' asked Marvin, uncertainly, looking to the woods either side.

'I'll call them,' Alex decided, putting his hand to his pocket. 'Oh! Ollie is calling now.'

Alex answered the phone.

'Haha, I was just about to buzz you, what's happened? Why is Ben in such a rush?'

Marvin placed a hand on Alex's shoulder to draw his attention.

'He's shouting something, listen.'

Alex lowered the phone, listening intently. Not much could be heard over the rain bashing the canopy of leaves around them.

'It sounds a bit like *run*?' he said, unsure.

He placed the phone to his ear again.

'Ollie? What's happened? Is Ben telling us to run?'

A high-pitched voice was already apparently talking down the line at the other end to a lullaby-like cadence.

'*Thirteen, Fourteen, Maids-a-courting,*
'*Fifteen, Sixteen, Maids in the kitchen,*
'*Seventeen, Eighteen, Maids in waiting,*
'*Nineteen, Twenty, My plate's empty.*'

HERETIC'S DESCENT

'Bólstadα,' whispered Jusic I'Lyr into the damp darkness of the Undercity sewers. It was a greeting of a language long dead, but one he knew would pander to the Oracle's eagerness to honour the Old Ones. A shuffle of feathers ahead of him suggested that he would at least be given an audience and out from the shadows crept the decrepit and unkept Avian.

'I did not know the Palace taught their young of languages long dead, Inquisitor I'Lyr,' the Oracle croaked, the words jagged and rough as they slipped from his beak. A hacking dry cough followed which the Oracle stifled by turning his head into the coat of dusty green feathers that draped off his arms. Many were missing, bent or broken, noted Jusic, reflecting sadly on how majestic the emerald cloak once looked to him as a child.

'An education dependent entirely upon the Palace's teachings would leave more than just the knowledge of the Old Ones left undiscovered, I fear,' Jusic responded softly.

The Oracle clicked in agreement, his eyes darting around as if chasing the echoes.

'This place is a bit off the beaten path for you. Best we retreat somewhere more private, the eyes of the Undercity rarely sleep.'

'Indeed,' Replied Jusic solemnly, looking behind him as he placed a gentle hand on the shoulder of the Oracle, guiding him back into the shadowy alcove from where he emerged. The Undercity was a treacherous place for someone of Jusic's position to be discovered and he was more than aware of how his golden robes must stand out amongst the shades of black and green around him.

Once safe from view of the main strip, Jusic leaned his quarterstaff against the wall and began to kneel before the Oracle.

'Remain standing Inquisitor,' croaked the Oracle. 'We are hardly in the environment where such pageantry would be expected.'

Jusic straightened and nodded. 'Oracle, I appreciate that you may no longer wish to be sought out in this fashion, but I am in dire need of your council.'

The Oracle hobbled over to what was once a stone pillar, reclining onto the broken stump with the uncomfortableness of someone past their prime.

'Your words would suggest that you believe my exile to absolve me of my duty to the citizens of I Citadel, Inquisitor. That now I reside amongst the bandits and bastards that I too must reject my place and purpose in society?'

'No, not at all, please, take no offence with my choice of words.' Jusic raised his hands reassuringly, as if calming a wild animal. He knew all too well of the Oracle's erratic temperament and was careful not to clash with him this early into the conversation.

'I simply meant that you may not wish to help my kind any further after being treated as you have.'

The Oracle nodded, apparently happy with the explanation.

'I thank you for the concern, but I know the decision to cast me out was that of The Prince alone and not of the vox populi.

For those who are willing to risk their freedom in the attempt to reach me here, I will endeavour to help where I can.'

He leaned forward to Jusic now, his black eyes somehow illuminated in the dimly lit alcove. He continued, quieter than before.

'But your arrival does concern me somewhat, Inquisitor. Were the word to reach the Palace that one of its Royal Guard was down here with me, I am not sure the resulting scandal would leave either of us with much to live for. So, either The Prince has sent you here to finish me off, or what is troubling you is of great importance.'

'Surely you would know if I were here to kill you.' Jusic replied, half in jest.

'My kind cannot see the future, Inquisitor, nor do we profess to. We simply see the world through lenses different to your own.' The Oracle paused, as if the topic required no further elaboration, and then hunched over closer to Jusic as if to whisper. '…I need not my gifts as an Avian to know you pose no threat to me on this day, however, as otherwise you would have kept a better eye on this majestic quarterstaff…'

Jusic's eyes darted to the wall where his weapon no longer lay, snapping back to face the Oracle to find the Avian casually using the golden staff to lean forwards towards him on his seat.

'…Troubles of great importance it is then,' said the Oracle, his beak clicking gently.

Jusic smiled briefly before letting out a deep sigh.

'I am afraid, Oracle. I am afraid I no longer believe in the direction our civilisation is heading under The Prince's rule.'

'And what direction is that exactly?'

Jusic glanced away from the obsidian black eyes before him to the wall behind, as if it made the confession easier to say aloud.

'We used to be a noble and altruistic race... scouring the skies for those like us and offering liberty and prosperity to the creatures and cultures we found amongst the Dark Wastes.'

Jusic shook his head bitterly, as if fighting the word. 'But I fear the offer becomes more of a poisoned chalice with each new discovery. It has become hard to ignore the fires of nationalism being stoked by The Prince of late. Those we welcome are no longer treated with the respect that our forefathers envisioned when they sent us into the stars. Many of the newer races are nothing more than slaves to the established.'

The Oracle nodded softly. This wasn't news to him, thought Jusic. The Avian's expulsion from the Uppercity had been as a result of The Prince's purge of all things *alien* to his pureblood-orientated vision. Jusic took the pause to look past the Oracle at his new surroundings, a far cry from the opulent Temple of Sight he inhabited above.

The clunk of his quarterstaff gently dropping from a small height snapped Jusic back to meet the Oracle's gaze, where the Avian clicked his beak in thought.

'Somewhere beyond the sights of this Citadel,' began the Oracle, his words careful and deliberate, 'spins a very unremarkable planet, isolated in a sleepy and insignificant galaxy. When we will come across this planet, I cannot say, but I would suggest that you decide upon your thoughts on The Prince prior to this moment.'

The Oracle clicked his beak again, something behind his dark eyes was swirling. Vague whispers escaped his beak, but not directed to Jusic. Were it a language of sorts, it was not one he knew.

'I caution you though, Inquisitor,' he continued louder, now in the common tongue. 'Because while I cannot say with certainty that this will be the case, it seems likely that your actions on this day could result in the fall of the Citadel as we know it. An unfair burden for anyone, I daresay, but one you may have to carry no less.'

The Oracle bowed his head slightly, drumming his fingers on the quarterstaff impatiently, as if agitated by his own words. 'I don't know what waits beyond this, the possibilities are too vast and volatile to decrypt.'

'No,' Jusic retorted, flatly.

'No...?' The Oracle didn't appear surprised by his response.

'No, that is not a position I am looking to be in. I do not wish to go against The Prince, I simply just want a return to our roots!' said Jusic exasperated. 'What does this fall even mean? Are you telling me the Citadel will collapse? Fall from the Wastes? I will not be responsible for the deaths of the billions that call this place home. No, this is not why I came to you.'

'Those answers are not ones I can or wish to answer. All I will say to you is to think carefully about where your moral line sits in regard to The Prince's actions, because it appears a time will come where you will have to evaluate just how loyal you are to him.'

Jusic rose to continue arguing, but the Oracle cut him off before he could speak.

'...It is time for you to leave, Inquisitor. In but a few moments, one of your colleagues from the Palace will be passing through these sewers in search of someone to sell him his unsightly Ethexric Powder. If you do not leave now you will be spotted.'

The arrival of this mystery colleague seemed very fortuitous to prevent further discussion, thought Jusic, but he bowed with respect nonetheless and made a swift exit.

Navigating the sewers of the Undercity with haste, Jusic caught a flick of a familiar gold cloak far towards the west exit. When no confrontation came, Jusic assumed he had gone unnoticed himself and climbed one of the ladders to the hatch above.

The Citadel didn't sleep, but the atmosphere at this time was relatively quiet. It was hard to maintain a regular day/night cycle travelling through the stars and this was something the Commercial Quarter took advantage of. Dazzling neon lights and aggressive advertisements peppered the horizon, daring anyone to find something more interesting to look at.

Jusic strode forward with confidence into the bloom of light, as if on a nightly patrol. His thoughts however remained with the slums of the Undercity somewhere below his feet, the Oracle's words of caution sitting uncomfortably in his mind.

Present Day

'You are dismissed,' Jusic muttered casually, striding past the guards to the Citadel's Sanctum with little acknowledgment. Access to this room was limited to only the upper echelon of the Palace's guard and the flamboyant door Jusic had just flung apart helped, along with the guards, to cement the reputation to the public that what lay beyond was mysterious and secret.

In actuality, the room was quite minimalistic and plain by Citadel standards. Its main feature sat squarely in the room's centre: an array of translucent screens, each accompanied with various controls and blinking buttons. Other than a collection of trinkets and trophies from conquered cultures that adorned three of the four walls, nothing else was stored here. What did also perhaps aid the Sanctum with its alluring reputation was the fourth wall, which the central station faced. This wall was transparent and gave the occupants of the Sanctum a clear view over the Palace's Coliseum grounds.

The clinks of the guards descending the stairs behind him told Jusic that it was safe to seal the doors. Moving towards one of the screens in the centre, he did so with a few taps of his finger. Security within the Sanctum hadn't always been so tight, reflected Jusic, in recent years however The Prince had decreed that critical operation rooms be continuously guarded unless occupied by high-ranking officials, of which Jusic fortunately was one.

'There is a distinct lack of chairs in this room,' came a sharp voice from the corner to his right. Jusic looked up from the screen to see that he was already joined by The Three Sisters.

'Chairs encourage complacency,' Jusic said, absently, tapping into the terminal in the middle. He let his response linger for a moment before glancing in The Sisters' direction, smiling at the stony expressions that met him. '...Or at least, that is the latest musing from our great Lord, which I obviously, whole-heartedly, support.' He placed a hand to his chest and winked.

Before The Sisters could rebuke, Jusic straightened and stepped towards a side wall. 'Have you three ever come across the Tetradonites in your travels?'

'Uh, Tetradonites...' mumbled The Sister Ashren, looking up in recollection. 'No, I believe they died out some time ago, Jusic, or at least there are none left in the Citadel as I can recall.'

'A pity,' Jusic said heavily, picking up a small white rectangular cuboid from the shelf in front of him. 'The Tetradonites were a marvellous set of beings, very brilliant and resourceful.'

'I don't think I've ever even seen a Tetradonite,' said The

Sister Tiki, looking to the other two uncertainly, before addressing Jusic again. 'What did they look like?'

'They were mostly marine in nature, Tiki, you would recognise one I imagine if you had crossed paths. Big eyes and gills, often wet. Actually if they weren't wet they were in trouble. A passive race though, but importantly, they could swell and balloon their usually small bodies to incredible sizes when required. It made housing them aboard the Citadel somewhat of an architectural challenge back in the day.'

Jusic walked over to The Sisters and placed the cuboid down on the floor before the window in front of them.

'If the other guards knew we were getting race history lessons in addition to front row "standing space" to a Trial, gosh, they would be green with envy,' remarked the last sister, Vhe, sarcastically.

Jusic smiled. 'Oh, I'm sorry, Vhe, did you not want somewhere to sit?'

The Sisters all looked down to the small cuboid before them. It was no bigger than the daggers The Sisters wore upon their belts.

'Mmm, I'm not convinced we will all squeeze on this,' Vhe said dryly.

'Aha, right you are, Vhe, right you are. You almost certainly could not fit upon this in its current state.' Jusic flicked his cloak and unclipped his golden quarterstaff from his waist. It glistened, reflecting the lights in the room, the golden orb on top sending an array of refracted light around the four of them. He delicately placing the orbed end to the surface of the cuboid. '...But if you had let me ramble, I would have explained that the Tetradonites miraculously invented material to expand and contract to reflect their proportional need at the time.'

At the touch of the quarterstaff, the cuboid shuddered

and expanded rapidly, as if made from foam. The rectangular shape remained sharp and defined as it grew until, suddenly, a perfectly shaped bench sat between The Sisters and the window.

Jusic knew expecting gasps of shock or incredulities from The Sisters was perhaps a tall order. So he settled for the faint nod of approval from Ashren.

'I'm sure I need not mention the requirement to keep this little trinket a secret between us four,' he said, being the first to take a seat. 'I told The Prince that the item was a whetstone from the ancient Kaphalonians.'

The Sisters tentatively sat down beside him, surprised at the bench's ability to hold their weight considering how effortlessly it had expanded.

Ashren was the first to speak.

'Jusic, why have you invited us into the Sanctum today? I am not aware of any of the other inquisitors' house guards being allowed access to a live Trial?'

Jusic looked to Ashren, then Tiki and Vhe, acknowledging the curious expression they each held. He understood their confusion.

'Do you remember much of your life before the Polox Plague of 781?' he asked, aware of the fact he wasn't immediately answering their question. Luckily, The Sisters had known him long enough to trust that this tangent would lead to a point – hopefully.

'Not much,' Vhe said, bluntly, clearly fighting the urge to just insist on an answer to Ashren's original question.

'We were many back then,' Tiki responded, solemnly. 'Many Sisters.'

'You were,' agreed Jusic, nodding. 'The Serpentines were a tenacious addition to the Citadel at the time. Ferocious and formidable. Your kind would have likely become one of the dominant houses had the plague not occurred.'

Vhe sighed, running her fingers across her temples.

'Where is this leading, Jusic, please?'

'Sweet Vhe, your patience shames your ancestors,' he said with a twinkle in his eye. 'I am leading to just this. Ever since the plague, the Citadel's teachings often portray the Serpentines as a weakened breed, one that could fall to an invisible foe, such as a virus, which all others survived.'

Jusic looked to the expanse ahead in front of them, his gaze not focused on anything in particular. A touch of fragility entered his voice.

'I know the decision to employ you three as the head of my guard has upset and angered many. The very fact the Sanctum's guards did not leave until I arrived is testament to that. But you three, the sole survivors of your race, deserve far more respect than the Citadel will give you.'

He looked across to them, even Vhe hanging off his words now.

'Left to just the teachings, the history of the Serpentines will be of ruin and ridicule. I am eager for that not to be the case, not only for yourselves, but I fear we often overlook the value of the few and far between.'

Jusic ran his fingers across the surface of the cuboid bench as he spoke.

'We should not forget any of them,' he concluded, letting his words linger for a moment.

As if suddenly aware he was in the middle of a conversation, Jusic looked up and smiled to The Sisters.

'And that is why you are here today. It is long overdue for you three to assume a more prominent role in the Palace. Plus, I feel watching a Trial live gives an accurate picture of the cultures we are encountering. It's not as if anyone is going to argue with you being here, the halls still talk of the time Tiki handled that that riot down in Oldtown by herself.'

'Riot is too strong a word,' Tiki said, bashfully. 'There were only 12 of them.'

Jusic let out a hearty laugh and regarded The Sisters with a polite nod as he got up and returned to the terminal in the centre of the room.

After traversing the buttons and switches for several minutes, Jusic motioned to The Sisters to remain quiet, indicating he was about to send a communication.

'This is Inquisitor I'Lyr, Sanctum Terminal Officer for Trial #2925001. The Coliseum is prepared and ready for Collection. You have my authority to continue.'

A gravelled voice crackled through the terminal.

'Acknowledged, Inquisitor I'Lyr, commencing the Collection.'

Several lights upon the terminal flickered dark red, matching the walls of the Sanctum. Satisfied all was in hand, Jusic returned to the transparent pane in front of him and looked out over the Coliseum with The Sisters.

It was a sight he often approached with apprehension. The vast expanse before them was named appropriately – it was a colossal amount of space and distance. The Sanctum's window loomed many miles above the actual ground, just below the point where the Coliseum's own weather system might disrupt visibility.

The view often gave Jusic a sickening sense of vertigo and, had The Sisters not been in attendance on this day, Jusic likely would have turned the window opaque and watched the Trial from the terminal's live feed.

Instead, they all looked out and, for the first time in many years, Jusic watched as tiny little red lights flickered on around the Coliseum walls. Millions and millions of these lights trickled up towards them, signalling that the Collection was underway. Before them soon became an ocean of red as it neared competition, the brown sandy floor of the Coliseum appearing smaller and smaller against the oppressive hues of the lights.

Jusic glanced up and watched as the lights flowed up towards the ceiling, becoming obscured by the now bur-gundy clouds. It was not often a population exceeded past the Sanctum's window, but it was known to happen on occasion.

'How do they watch?' Tiki asked, also examining the clouds above.

'There are screens in their capsules which display the Coliseum and the Trial,' responded Jusic. 'Not dissimilar to our own window here.'

He wrapped his knuckles against the glass.

'Maybe ours is a screen also,' pondered Vhe, pressing her hand against the pane.

Jusic chuckled. 'A good point, perhaps you should dive through and test that theory, Vhe.'

She scowled in Jusic's direction, as she did, the red gradient reflecting on the side of her face suddenly switched to a brilliant white, forcing her hand off the glass to cover her eyes from the brightness before them.

'What has happened?' she asked, alarmed.

Jusic had turned his back and was making his way towards the terminal again.

'The Collection is complete, Vhe, the creatures of this planet are now all accounted for and contained,' he said, tapping away at the terminal once more. 'Temporarily, at least,' he added.

'What do we know of this planet, Jusic?' Ashren inquired, her eyes becoming accustomed to the blinding light of the Coliseum.

'The planet itself is quite healthy, Ashren, by all accounts, the creatures themselves however...'

Vhe piped up.

'I heard a rumour that they are just talking meat?'

'Vhe, that's very derivative, imagine someone saying of the Serpentines that you are just walking lizards.'

'What is a *lizard*?' Vhe spat, undecided as to whether to be insulted or not.

Jusic only smiled before continuing.

'These creatures have an interesting lifecycle. Most spend their lives encased in their habitats, built by the workers before them. Occasionally, they have been known to adorn a metallic husk for terrain transversal and only in limited situations do they spend any time between the two.'

'What of religion?' asked Tiki.

Jusic screwed up his face, reviewing the text in front of him.

'It appears mixed, not the easiest bunch to accommodate for that's for sure. Many have individual shrines to what appears to be a porcelain deity within their habitat, which we can only presume is the prevailing religion, but this doesn't appear ever discussed amongst them or mentioned within more obvious places of worship.'

Ashren took in the scale of the Coliseum before her, now a pillar of bright white light, the roof above them obscured by clouds with the ground only just visible beneath them. Whether deliberate or not, the environment gave off an almost heavenly atmosphere. 'How has a champion been chosen to talk on their behalf?'

'I would love to say with great care and consideration, but the creatures appear so aggressive and divided that finding a unified voice was fruitless. So, we did the sensible thing and chose at random, hoping for the best.'

'Random?!' Ashren said incredulously. 'So you've given the responsibility to make a decision on behalf of a whole civilisation to just one of them, at random?'

'Indeed,' Jusic responded indifferently, continuing to tap away at the terminal.

'Isn't that a huge risk?' Ashren pressed.

'It could be, and often has been,' accepted Jusic, pausing momentarily. 'I trust that the fates will choose a suitable champion amongst these creatures however.'

'I dislike the word *creatures*, we should give them an official name if there is a chance they may be joining the Citadel, Jusic,' Tiki said peering down at the Coliseum floor.

'What about *Meatbag*-ians?' Vhe said flippantly, ignoring the exasperated look from Tiki.

'Porcelanians may be appropriate, if that is their chosen god,' pondered Ashren.

'It appears...' interjected Jusic, '...that they have developed an advanced writing and speech structure. This is fortunate, not only because it will make the actual Trial a little more engaging and easier to follow, but it should also give us an indication on what they call themselves.' Jusic scanned the page further, looking for the appropriate line.

'Aha, *humans*, apparently. Well, humans, welcome to the Citadel,' he said, pushing a large button to his right.

The Coliseum

Lupita was blinded by the light.

All she could feel beneath her was abrasion, a scratching sensation on her legs suggested she must be on her hands and knees. Slowly, the brightness receded, exposing a warm beige below her that she assumed to be that of a sandy floor.

It wasn't immediately clear how far the ground stretched, but as her eyes adjusted, Lupita began to pick out the boundary surrounding her.

Wherever this is, it's big, she thought to herself, taking in the circular arena through squinting eyes.

It certainly was large, a couple of football pitches at least, and that was just the floor span. As Lupita dragged her eyes up the walls, the majestic sandstone pillars surrounding her soon faded into a sea of nondescript brightness. Above her was the same, the wisps of what could be clouds barely visible against the oppressive white light.

Am I dead…? she thought, confused. What had happened? She was just walking to work and…

'No, Child, you are not dead.'

The voice was booming, yet crisp, erupting out of nowhere.

Lupita startled, scrambling off her knees backwards away from, well, presumably the voice. It was only through the abruptness of this manoeuvre that Lupita noticed she was wrapped mostly in what appeared to be white linen. A bodice of wraps covering her top half and single shoulder, with a more robe like attribute at the bottom. This wasn't what she was wearing just moments ago.

Panic, initially ignored by the overwhelming curiosity and absurdity of the situation, was beginning to set in.

Where was she?

'Forgive me,' the voice endured, cutting through the atmosphere as if Lupita were surrounded by invisible speakers. She looked for a source to the voice, but all she could see was sand and white light.

'This must be confusing for you, Child, I stress not to be concerned, you are safe. We have arrived.'

Above where the sandstone pillars faded into the brightness, colours began to dance and coalesce in the air. A visible bust began to form above her, a translucent hologram of sorts, revealing presumably the owner of the imposing voice.

'I am known as The Prince,' claimed the top half of a regal looking man above her, his appearance filling the skies of the circular tower. 'You have been chosen, Lupita.'

Chosen? What does that mean? thought Lupita, continuing to be utterly perplexed.

'I must inform you, that, while I can hear your thoughts clearly at this moment, those watching our exchange, cannot. I would ask that you speak verbally, for their benefit.'

'I…' Lupita stammered with her words, not knowing what to say, or even how loud she needed to project her voice to be heard. The bust of The Prince loomed above her and as her eyes continued to adjust, his features became more apparent. The Prince was pale, perhaps as a result of the white light, with sharp cheek bones and an angular, roman nose. The crown on his head was lavish and opulent. He wore it with a posture that suggested he wore the extravagance with pride, no matter how impractical it must be to wear.

After a moment's reflection, Lupita found her voice.

'…Who is watching us?' she asked tentatively, but audibly.

'A fabulous first question,' regarded The Prince with a curt smile, 'and one that provides an excellent introduction.' The image of The Prince raised his arms to gesture at the cylindrical walls surrounding them above.

'You have the privilege of being watched by your entire species, Child. They watch from the lights spanning the totality of this Coliseum.'

Lupita scanned the skies, immediately daunted by the prospect of a trillion eyes on her.

Is this a nightmare? she questioned herself without thinking.

The Prince did not address the question, presumably for the benefit of those watching.

'We have brought you here, your species, to the Citadel. I have done this to save you.'

'To save us from what exactly?' she returned.

'Another excellent question, Child, Th…'

'I am no Child,' interrupted Lupita decisively, brushing

133

off the sand from her knees as she stood, facing The Prince's face that loomed above her.

The Prince hesitated only slightly, clearly surprised at the defiance. A flash of irritation crossed what could be seen of his face before disappearing, a fake smile instantly redressed upon it as if amused by the challenge.

'Alas, but you are all children of the Citadel once upon our ship,' he clarified, pausing. 'But if you would prefer, for the time being, I will address you as Lupita.'

As if satisfied by his own diplomacy, the image of The Prince clasped his hands together and bowed in slightly. 'But to answer your question, this is to save you from yourselves, ultimately.'

Lupita let this statement rest while she considered her response. The grains of sand beneath her feet felt too real, too coarse, for this to be a dream. The white linen wraps, while soft, provided a tactile reminder that she was not having an out-of-body experience either. The so-called 'Prince' had exhibited a shade of emotion when she had interrupted him earlier, perhaps this was something she could work with.

She didn't know exactly why she felt so defiant, it wasn't necessarily in her nature. Lupita quietly reflected on what she was feeling. Behind the confusion, the bewilderment, she sensed a wisp of anger bubbling away. Resentment at being placed in such an exposed and confusing situation, allegedly in front of the entire human race. She didn't dwell on it long, it was evident The Prince could read her thoughts in some capacity, so she blinded the discovery of this wrath with a reel of other emotions. Uncertainty, intimidation, insecurity. Was The Prince familiar enough with human psychology that he could tell an artificial thought from a real one? She quickly decided to play the part he clearly wanted her to play, falling to her knees once more in apparent submission, overwhelmed.

Exhibiting a broad, caring and in its own way, synthetic, smile, The Prince soon answered this.

'I understand the fear and hesitation you will be battling with. Know you are not the first to stand on these sacred sands and you must take solace in that it will be here, on this day, that you, Lupita, will bring salvation and safety to your people.'

The Prince seemed intent on steering this conversation to a question around what exactly 'her people' needed to be saved from, as if following a set script. How often had he done this? Aware that she had just asked herself a question that The Prince undoubtedly could interpret, she looked up expectantly for a response.

The translucent Prince loomed, pressing down an expectant stare upon Lupita, but he did not answer her hidden question.

Interesting, thought Lupita, *this show isn't just for me then. This is a performance of sorts.*

The wisps of anger danced away deep inside her. She felt them building, but quickly distracted herself. In this situation where her own thoughts were not secure, she needed something up her sleeve at least.

'Why me?' Lupita asked aloud, deliberately avoiding the obvious question he wanted her to ask and with hopefully a believable meekness to her voice.

Many would have easily missed the brief quiver in The Prince's eyelids. A subtle squint of sorts that suggested that this wasn't going how he had hoped. Lupita caught it however, a small victory at the very least.

Composing himself quickly, The Prince lifted his head and arms, speaking broadly to the audience of lights around them once again.

'Yes, why *you?*' he echoed.

135

The Sanctum

'They are really just meatbags then,' concluded Vhe, looking through the window and down to the coliseum floor below. She could just make out Lupita through the holographic crown that dominated their view from above. 'Soft, squishy, meatbags.'

'Mmmm,' responded Jusic, his attention on the terminal in front of him.

Tiki cocked her head in thought as she watched The Prince gesture to the Coliseum.

'The human *does* appear quite unconvincing I guess, not particularly remarkable. Do they differ largely from their champion at all?'

Jusic remained glued to his screen, the suggestion of a frown etched into his brow.

'No, they are quite consistent,' he added after a slight delay. 'Different colours to their fur, different colours to their membranes, body proportions... that sort of normal variation. Nothing inherently important.'

He tapped away at some buttons, distracted. 'Could you let me know when the champion is being presented with her first memory please?'

'Memory? Do they get presented with their memories?' asked Tiki, looking up and around excitedly beyond the glass in front of her.

'It is part of the Trial,' answered Ashren, eyeing Jusic as he tapped away at his console with haste. 'The Prince likes to play back snippets of the champions' memories to inspire them to join the Citadel.'

'How would that work exactly?' Tiki pressed.

'It provides a couple of purposes really. Replaying specific memories in the coliseum can be both a demonstration to the species why the champion is worthy of talking on their behalf, whilst simultaneously incentivising the champion into agreeing to the Citadel's terms.'

'...Or to humiliate them into submission,' muttered Vhe, folding her arms and leaning against the glass. 'What better way to get compliance than to blackmail a champion with the suggestion you can show your entire race their darkest moments.'

Jusic stopped typing and looked up to Vhe, concerned.

'Careful,' he cautioned; his voice quiet. 'You must not be caught speaking in such a way.'

'What?!' defended Vhe with incredulity. 'Are you telling me that he does not use it for that purpose, Jusic?'

'I see it!' proclaimed Tiki, diffusing the atmosphere and pointing beyond to the Coliseum below. 'The hologram of The Prince has been replaced by a scene of sorts, it looks to be of a small human offspring.'

'Thank you, Tiki,' said Jusic, a noticeable weight to his words. 'I would kindly ask you three to remain quiet for a moment please.'

Vhe opened her mouth to question him, however a sharp, static noise interrupted her as one of the screens in front of Jusic came to life.

'Your Highness,' he reacted, instantly bowing.

'Inquisitor I'Lyr,' The Prince snarled. His voice considerably less of a majestic boom within the Sanctum walls. 'I presume you have requested my attention for a purpose?'

Jusic stood straight from his bow. 'Indeed, I have, my apologies, but we have a situation.'

The Sisters looked to each other silently from behind the terminal, out of sight.

'What kind of situation?' asked The Prince, pointedly.

'The Collection did not capture all the population it seems; one human inexplicably remains.'

If Jusic's news had alarmed The Prince, he didn't

immediately show it. However, his apparent composure was betrayed by his next words, that jumped from his mouth with striking venom and urgency.

'What do you mean, one remains? You will initiate the Collection again.'

'I have tried, your Highness, several times. They will not be summoned.'

'Then eliminate them,' spat The Prince, facetiously. 'I want that planet empty of life before this Trial is over, Inquisitor.'

'Understood, your Highness.'

'Send the Thrǣll to the planet on my authority immediately and I want an engineer to look over the Collection for signs of sabotage too.'

'An engineer has already been requested; I will mobilise the Thrǣll after this call.'

'This champion…' The Prince lingered, looking beyond the screen presumably to something that lay beyond him. 'She is going to be trouble, I'Lyr, there is a disobedience within her that could prove problematic.'

'Mmm, I saw,' acknowledged Jusic, 'I have faith the memories will placate her though.'

'And so they must, I wish not to be forced to take more direct preparations.' He let the ambiguity of his statement dissipate. 'You have your orders, Inquisitor; I want your next call to be of completion.'

The Prince disappeared, returning the room's natural red ambience to Jusic's profile.

After a short silence, Ashren stepped towards Jusic who had remained in place, contemplative.

'The Thrǣll, Jusic? What business do we have to summon those beasts anywhere?' A hint of anxiety was evident in her voice. 'Are they not normally used in times of war?'

Ashren's question snapped Jusic out of his trance, and he turned to The Sisters, giving a distant smile.

'Indeed, Ashren,' he said, circling the terminal with his arms behind his back, making towards them by the Sanctum's window. He looked down at the scene playing out below. Lupita was just visible through the dancing lights of another memory. The Coliseum was being shown a scene from her childhood, another little human was crying, being comforted by what appeared to be a young Lupita. Jusic tried to focus on Lupita's expression as she watched from below but they were up far too high to make out any detail. A mixture of captivation and horror most likely, he assumed.

'The Prince cannot take a chance in this regard,' he said, eventually. 'The Collection has never failed us before and we can't risk the planet remaining inhabited after the Trial of Lupita here.'

'Why not?' pressed Tiki, now looking down to the coliseum floor alongside Jusic. 'What risk does this one remaining human pose?'

Jusic lowered his voice ever so slightly.

'It is not the individual left on the planet that The Prince fears, Tiki.' He glanced across at The Sister, ensuring that his lowered tone was being heard. 'More a prophecy he once received around such an event.'

Ashren was the first to respond, brashly disregarding the drop in conversational volume.

'Prophecy?! What prophecy? There is no record of The Prince engaging with the Oracles.'

Jusic snapped his finger to his lips, hushing Ashren.

'I know,' continued Jusic in a whisper, 'and that is because, officially, The Prince never has.'

He raised his eyebrows and stared at The Sisters, highlighting the implication in his words. He chose his next ones with care.

'...But if such a situation were to occur, and The Prince

had received an unfavourable prophecy of sorts, potentially related to the continued habitation of a planet while a Trial occurred, I would imagine he would want that knowledge expunged from all records for risk of appearing capable of failure.'

Vhe held Jusic's stare and nodded slightly in acknowledgment. 'Did this have anything to do with the Oracle himself being exiled?' she asked.

'I couldn't possibly say – nor should we spend our energy on fables and mysteries, when there are Thrӕll to mobilise.'

Ashren shook her head, unsure.

'The Thrӕll though, Jusic, really? Send one of us to deal with this sole human. A legion of Thrӕll seems overkill.'

'We don't know enough of the human's capabilities at this point, Ashren,' Jusic returned, firmly. 'I will not risk sending you down there until we know more, besides, this is the very purpose of the Thrӕll, they are disposable to some extent. We can always make more.'

'Only from our dead,' Ashren reminded him, stepping up to Jusic. 'The morbidity of using them at all unsettles me, Jusic.'

Jusic wavered, looking to Ashren and the other Sisters.

'I know,' he said remorsefully, placing a compassionate hand upon Ashren's shoulder. 'It is not an action I take lightly, but one I must take regardless. I know many of the Thrӕll are your fallen kin themselves. Possibly, there is solace in the fact that even in death they fight on as Thrӕll to protect the Citadel and its inhabitants?'

'Is this protection?' Ashren asked, rhetorically, a pointedness to her words that Jusic was used to receiving from Vhe, not Ashren. 'Those monsters are no longer our kin, Jusic, they are soulless viruses masquerading in the bodies of our former brethren.'

Tiki spoke from behind Ashren.

'The Serpentine bodies amongst the Thræll should be put to rest at least, Jusic.'

'I have to agree,' said Vhe, still leaning against the glass behind her with arms folded. 'It is a disgrace to see Serpentines of old running around rabid and uncontrolled. It is not a respectful way to treat our dead.'

Jusic nodded solemnly, lowering his hands from Ashren. He afforded himself a glance down to Lupita, using the time to think, before returning to the centre of the room.

'I am, unfortunately, duty bound to carry out The Prince's wishes,' he said, moving past the terminal towards the wall of trinkets behind. 'But therein lies an opportunity...'

He trailed off, distracted. His eyes found an ornate scimitar that adorned a shelf near the top of the display.

'Were you ever taught of the Khappit Massacre in your teachings?' he asked, stepping forward to remove the scimitar from the wall, careful not to touch the blade's edge.

'Please, Jusic, not another lesson...' Vhe moaned, exasperated.

He ignored her, lost in his own thoughts.

'The Khappit were never a major house aboard the Citadel, but their numbers were vast, so much so that at one point nearly our entire Thræll army consisted of fallen Khappit.' He flipped the scimitar over in his hand, inspecting the blade with bored curiosity. The handle consisted of petrified wood, glimmers of bright opal amongst the grain.

'Anyway, in a similar vein to yourselves, a small group of Khappit took umbrage with the fact that the corpses of their brothers and sisters were being used as cannon fodder in the Citadel's wars. So, one night they snuck into the Thræll compound and cut one of the main water pipes with a scimitar not dissimilar to this one, flooding the entire compound. The Thræll, well, they lack the basic intelligence to swim or find higher ground, so they drowned, about half of the entire Thræll army was lost in a matter of hours.'

He placed the scimitar back on its perch carefully, turning to face The Sisters.

'Do you understand why I am telling you this?' he finished, hands clasped.

'Because… you want us to give the Thræll swimming lessons…?' Tiki responded slowly, only somewhat in jest.

'No,' Ashren added before Jusic could come in, her eyes on him carefully again as she spoke. 'No, he is saying that others before us have begrudged the use of their kinsfolk as undead Thræll.'

'Exactly.' Jusic nodded, encouragingly.

'But what does this have to do with this current situation?' asked Vhe, annoyed. 'Unless you plan for us to flood the planet when you send them down there?'

'No, but close,' lied Jusic, not wanting to deter Vhe and risk her engagement in the conversation. With a quick check behind him to the closed doors of the Sanctum, he lowered his eyes again. 'But what if I were to send you down to the planet under the illusion of ensuring that the human is dealt with, all the while providing you ample opportunity to… allow those of your race, and others –should you chose to – to find the peace they deserve?'

He looked to each Sister, gauging their reaction. Tiki was the first to speak.

'I love it,' she said, eagerly pulling out the daggers from her satchel. 'Let's do it.'

'Hold on, wait,' said Vhe, ushering Tiki's hands down in reluctance. 'Are you sure, Jusic? What happened to the Khappit after their actions?'

'Oh they were all massacred, hence the name. Sadly, this included even those who had nothing to do with the Thræll compound incident, The Prince purged them all.' He hoped the bitterness in his voice was well hidden. 'This is different, however. The only person monitoring the planet is currently me, and The Prince will be too distracted with the Trial to take notice. Providing you only kill a small number that could reasonably be blamed on the remaining human, there will be no cause for suspicion.'

'And what of the human?' queried Ashren.

Jusic hesitated before answering, weighing the options.

'Perhaps keep it alive for as long as you can justify your activity down there, and then just leave it to it,' he said, indifferently.

The Sisters looked to each other, this time measuring their own reactions. After a moment, an earnest agreement was evident between them.

'But, Jusic,' whispered Tiki, cautiously drifting her daggers back to her hip. 'What we talk of is dangerous, can The Prince not read minds?'

'Aha, a wise consideration,' he said, returning to the terminal to type his instructions to deploy the Thrǣll to the planet. 'The Prince only has one Seer left after he exiled the Avians, and that one will be entirely focused on reading the champion's mind down there.' He nodded to the Coliseum beyond the window.

After a few extra flourished taps of the terminal, Jusic stood back resolute and satisfied.

'The Thrǣll are being sent to the planet now and I've attached an auditable instruction that I am sending my house guards to oversee the operation. I suggest you head to Deployment quickly, I'm not sure how much time you will have.'

The Sisters turned to leave, an eager haste to their steps.

'I'll monitor you from up here as best I can, be discreet and be careful,' he added, watching them pass through the door to descend down the stairs. A small wave of Tiki's wielded dagger behind them was as much of a goodbye as he was to expect.

As the door softly shut after them, leaving Jusic alone in the Sanctum, he paced around the terminal once more to look out of the transparent pane of glass that separated him from the Coliseum. An uncomfortable thought bubbled up inside him, repressed and forgotten words from his own visit to an Avian all those years ago.

No, he said, reassuring himself, *that day is not today.*

The scene being broadcast below had switched to a later memory, it appeared, Lupita was older now and in a learning setting. Other young humans were laughing in her direction, while the image of a young Lupita herself sunk into a chair, clearly mortified for some reason. Jusic then noticed a holographic puddle that dripped below the chair the youth sat in. Through the memory, Jusic tried to focus on the adult Lupita watching below from the Coliseum floor. She stood stoic and unwavering as she watched what was clearly a painful memory.

He's trying to manipulate you, he said to himself, willing the thought down to Lupita below. *Stay strong.*

Earth

Lin was confused as to why everything was sideways. It wasn't until he sensed the cold earth on the right side of his face that he realised he was lying on the ground.

Baffled, he pushed himself up and looked around, comforted to find himself still in the gardens of Albert Park.

What happened? Did I have a stroke or something?

Something wasn't right with that explanation however; the park was a hive of activity when he was out walking the pram just moments ago, now, it was empty and the sky appeared much darker, so if he did have a stroke and had been here a while why didn't someone hel…

Oh god – Jasper!

Lin jumped to his feet and dived towards the pram by his side, feeling instantly sick.

It was empty.

Acidic panic burst inside Lin.

'JASPER!' he cried out, looking around desperately.

He scanned the various discarded items around the park for signs of movement.

Nothing.

He looked to the rows of trees surrounding the field.

Nothing.

His eyes passed over a large picnic and collection of discarded bicycles.

Nothi—

Hmm, bit of an odd thing to leave at the park, he thought momentarily to himself.

'JASPER!' he called out again, spinning around.

The panic was now transitioning to nauseating dread. Lin pushed the pram over erratically, checking under the carriage in desperation.

'JASPER!'

Why is there so much debris and rubbish left here though?

Lin was infuriated at himself for even contemplating the environmental littering at a time like this.

What the fuck is wrong with me?

'HELP SOMEONE PLEASE, MY SON – JASPER! JASPER!'

But now he thought of it, there was more than just picnics and bicycles which looked out place here. There were coats and jackets strewn across the grass, balls and toys left unattended. What really caused Lin to pause however was the presence of other abandoned prams dotted around the field.

What on earth is going on her—

Movement. Lin saw movement. Ahead of him through the far line of trees. A figure was shaded and hard to see in the limited light, but someone was there.

'HELLO! HELP, CAN YOU HELP? MY SON, I CAN'T FIND MY SON!'

The silhouette shifted at his cries and Lin saw it stumbling slowly towards the source of Lin's disturbance.

Something is still wrong here, he decided, cautiously watching as the figure lumbered erratically towards him, hastily increasing its speed.

It was now that Lin noticed other shapes emerging from the treeline, each heading towards him with a noticeable stagger, as if they were not familiar with the length of their legs.

He looked to the pram by his side one last time, just in case he had missed something, some sign of where Jasper could be.

The figures were getting close enough now that Lin could make out the details of their appearance. There was little consistency in body shape between them, a few were large and bulking while some of the others were scrawny and slight. Some even resembled shapes that didn't make sense to Lin.

Was that… fur?

Despite these differences, all of them hobbled unpredictably, with greater and greater urgency towards Lin. He could now see their faces and the previous dread he felt transitioned once more into a guttural, primal terror. Their faces were of nothing Lin could recognise or register, absent in expression and what appeared like rabid foam oozing sinisterly from gaping mouths. Their skin, or in some cases hide, was dark mottled grey, decaying and flayed in places, eyes milky white.

'EXCUSE ME!' Lin shouted, unsure as to what to do.

'PLEASE CAN SOMEONE HELP, I THINK I'M HAVING A STROKE OR SOME MENTAL EPISODE.' Perhaps this was it, maybe he was unwell. The figures were close enough now that he didn't need to shout and Lin started backing away, checking behind him.

'Look, please, if anyone can hear me, nothing makes sense, don't come near me, I'm clearly not well.'

Closer they stumbled.

'Please come no closer, can someone call an ambulance? If anyone can hear me – I'm not well, please don't approach me. I don't want to hurt anyone!'

Closer.

Lin continued to retreat cautiously. He tried one last time, now talking beyond the approaching horde.

'IF ANYONE CAN HEAR ME, MY SON, JASPER, PLEASE FIND HIM AND MAKE SURE HE IS SAFE. HE HAS BLACK HAIR AND WAS WEARING A DINOSAUR TOP AND...'

Lin's trailing ankle caught the wheel of a discarded bicycle and he fell awkwardly over the frame backwards. As his back and head hit the ground, he noticed the sky didn't look quite right, but now was not the time to inspect additional problems. He rolled onto his front sharply and jumped up, hoisting the bike with him in the hopes of putting a barrier between him and *them*.

Only, the figures were no longer approaching. They lay around not far from him, some motionless, some spasming, thick black liquid oozing into the earth from apparent wounds.

Lin looked up and around for an explanation, slowly lowering the bike to the ground. With a precautionary hand still on the handlebars, he rubbed his eyes and temples with the other, frustrated and confused.

Nothing is making sense.

A rustle to his left alerted him, friend or foe?

Another figure was emerging from the tree line, similar to the others. This one was also careering towards him, increasing its speed as the others had despite the uneven gait.

Foe.

Lin made a snap decision and mounted the bike in front of him, giving one last longing look to the pram he was about to abandon.

'I will find you, Jasper,' he said aloud, but really to himself.

Setting off in the opposite direction, Lin tried not to focus on the plethora of movement he could see emerging around him.

The exit to the park looked clear and he thrashed towards it at full speed. Shadows shifted and surfaced in his direction, but he ignored them and focused on the escape.

Get to work, Lin told himself, concentrating. *Get to work and bunker down.*

Erogen Forensics wasn't far from the park, two roads' distance at most. It wasn't the military barracks he would have ideally wanted right now, but it was secure, more so than most places he could think of in the immediate area.

The streets were unsurprisingly empty as Lin burst through the park gate. Like the picnics and bicycles, cars littered the roads, abandoned mid-journey. Some had rolled into the paths and bushes ahead, while one he passed still had its indicator ticking ominously.

Lin turned down a road and risked a glance behind him, regretting it instantly. Several of the figures were galloping after him, spittle and froth flying behind them from their jagged and barbed mouths. In the light of the streetlights, he could see them snapping their jaws towards him in anticipation. Lin faced forward again and threw as much power into his legs as he could, surging onward, thighs burning.

The more he thought about it, the more the forensics labs made sense. The building had a firearms cabinet, he had worked on a handgun earlier this week in fact. Others would be in there too, rifles maybe, and importantly, ammunition. It was robust and protected, barbed wire lining the walls and heavy security doors guarding the labs inside. Crucially though, should anyone find Jasper, they would know where to find him.

Perhaps he didn't need a military barracks after all.

Lin skidded around the next corner at high speed, careful not to topple. Movement between the houses either side tried to lure his attention, but he kept pedalling forward, resolute, pretending he wasn't bothered by the shifting shadows on the roofs ahead of him.

He knew any movement wouldn't be Jasper. His best chance to see him again would be to get to work and get his head around this mess.

The compound was fast approaching, and Lin took a sharp turn to head towards the back entrance. He hadn't planned on coming into work on a weekend, so access through the front without his key card would be difficult. The back, though, provided a number pad option, meant for the night security manager to access the site. Lin just hoped he remembered the code.

Skidding to a stop outside the unit, Lin threw the bike behind him as a desperate barrier.

They were close.

Lin handled the keypad and frantically tried to remember the correct numbers.

Was it 1611*?

He punched them in, turning the handle.

No movement.

Christ what was the code? 1610*?

149

Again, nothing.

The sound of the bike being dragged behind him alerted him to the imminent danger and Lin dived to the left just as one of the scrawnier figures threw itself into the door where he had just stood.

Lin watched in horror as the beast writhed and growled in confusion, snapping its jaw loudly revealing impossibly sharp teeth. The beast spun frantically before noticing Lin lying immobilised in fear on the floor next to it.

It dived towards him.

Reactively, Lin heaved the discarded bike frame next to him between them, catching the thrashing, salivating monster just short of Lin's neck. It didn't seem to understand why it couldn't reach to bite him, snarling angrily and inching its teeth closer and closer.

The smell of what seemed like rotting flesh was overpowering, and Lin had to fight not only the strength of the savage animal on top of him but also the urge to just give up and accept that long good night.

Jasper.

Lin could not give up though, not even against such overwhelming hostility. Not until he found Jasper. He took the opportunity of the beast's confusion to look for a solution. His eyes landing on the spokes of the bike's wheels buffeting the side of his head.

Without thinking it through, Lin grabbed a spoke and snapped it from the wheel. The beast tried to snap at his exposed wrist but, as it did, Lin rammed the thin metal rod up through the beast's mouth into, hopefully, its brain.

With a quiver, the beast slumped and relaxed, mouth oozing with residual foam.

Lin didn't waste any time, he hauled the surprisingly dense monster from atop him and kicked the bike aside to stand once again in front of the keypad.

1609*, he tried.

Nothing – *fuck*!

Lin looked behind him hopelessly. At least three other beasts were charging towards him from across the carpark, clicking and gargling loudly like a war cry. A fourth and fifth were climbing over cars at the far end.

This was it; it was over.

Jasper.

Lin returned one last time to face the door and punched in one final attempt.

1612*.

He squeezed the handle tightly and turned, greeted with a satisfying clunk of metal moving. With a disbelieving eagerness, Lin tore the door towards him and slipped in the gap created, snatching at the bar on the other side before throwing the door closed behind.

The Sisters watched from a far building as Lin barricaded himself inside.

'Close one, that,' narrated Tiki, wiping the Thrǽll blood from her blades onto the bottom of her shoes. 'Didn't think he was going to make it.'

Ashren bobbed her head in agreement. 'Me either actually, we might have more time here than we thought. Didn't feel like helping him with the little one, Vhe?'

Vhe didn't respond right away.

'I wanted to see how he handled himself.'

'And?'

'Passable, for a bag of meat. The real test will be when he wants to leave this big box.'

The Sisters moved their attention back to the Thrǽll, jumping from the rooftop to ambush a few of the last remaining Serpentine undead.

The Coliseum

Lupita felt hollow.

She watched up, pained, as another familiar scene started to coalesce in the sky above her.

Maybe this was hell after all.

A now young adult Lupita was pushing forward the door into a dilapidated thrift shop, the little bell above the entrance only just managing to ding with her arrival.

Rows of old clothes greeted her, hanging limply from inconsistent and mismatching hangers. Lupita picked out an aisle of coats and strode towards it. A woman was already browsing the selection and she looked up as Lupita arrived.

'Lulu!' the woman proclaimed, excited.

Lupita hated being called Lulu, but put on a fake smile nonetheless.

'Jessica…!'

'Oh my god, it's been so long!'

'I know, how long has it been since school?'

'Six years, can you believe it?!'

Lupita could.

'No. You're kidding!'

'I'm not, I'm not, wow doesn't time fly! Feels like yesterday doesn't it?'

Remorseful that she did not choose a different shop to spend her lunch hour in, Lupita nodded in agreement. She very much wanted to avoid talking about her school years if she could, unfortunately despite being in separate social groups in those formative days, they were well beyond the point where Lupita could just pretend she didn't recognise her.

'How have you been anyway?' Jessica pressed, keen for the connection, or gossip, Lupita wasn't sure. 'What do you do these days?'

'Oh well primarily I bartend at the King's Arms down in Broadway but actually today I'm working a shift at the local school, just here on my lunch break actually.'

She hoped that the concluding statement might deter further conversation. It did not.

'Wow two jobs, I admire the hustle, Lulu, I wish I had your drive!'

Lupita just smiled, thumbing the second hand coat between her fingers awkwardly.

Jessica, perhaps not picking up on obvious social cues, continued.

'That's probably why you are here actually, snooping for some bargains! I love it, you know living frugally gives me such a rush. I mean sure we can go out and buy the next Louis Vuitton and such but why waste the money? Sometimes there is a diamond in the rough in these establishments.'

She gestured to the shop around her, at this point, Lupita noticed a man a few aisles along stuffing items into the pockets of his hoody.

'Indeed,' Lupita agreed, distracted. 'Excuse me a moment, Jessica.'

She stepped out towards the solitary till at the back of the building, where an aging cashier stood sorting out the day's receipts. Lupita had visited this shop enough to have picked out his accent before and so risked conversing with him in Nigerian to keep their conversation private.

'Watch out for the man by the shoes, he is stealing items in his jumper.'

The cashier looked up, startled to hear someone in his native tongue, his eyes flicking beyond Lupita to the thief. He nodded and thanked her quietly in Nigerian also.

'Oh my god you learnt a second language too!'

Jessica was now behind her, her arms laden with a stained fur coat for purchasing. 'Honestly, Lulu what's your secret?

Multi-lingual, side-hustles, upcycling old clothes… can we swap lives?!'

The memory evaporated from view with the echo of Jessica's laugh, replaced just like the others had been with the enigmatic return of The Prince.

'Can you not see, Lupita?' he bellowed, once again addressing the Coliseum's audience rather than Lupita directly. 'This is why you have been chosen as mankind's champion. Your compassion, your empathy, your constitution! With these, you embody the traits we see as intrinsically human.'

Lupita said nothing. Her knees wanted to buckle beneath her, just sink into the sand and never resurface. The Prince was leading to something, she was sure of it, and undoubtedly it would be revealed whether she responded or not.

This show seemed to go on regardless of her cooperation.

The wick of boldness she had initially felt had now been all but snuffed out, like a candle in a hurricane of traumatising and problematic recollections.

'And it is with this, Lupita, that I say to you. Choose survival. Allow me to bestow on you the title as leader of the humans. Lead them, as their champion, into the light of the Citadel. Accept our terms and amongst our civilisation you will live in harmony with galactic peers, equals, as we preserve intelligent life in this universe together, and unified. Accept me as your ruler and I shall look after you as my own.'

This speech again wasn't really for Lupita's benefit, made clear by the way The Prince spoke to the surrounding white lights rather than her.

'We already have leaders, elected leaders, why not them?' she muttered, the weight of this responsibility pressing down on her.

She was just nobody.

The Prince smiled broadly, a sickening smile that did not reflect in the eyes that peered soullessly from the artificial illusion above.

'We have seen your leaders. Observed them, their territorial ambitions, their nationalistic tendencies,' he said, sharing a serious, intimidating, expression to the Coliseum walls. 'Such attributes are toxic to our collective destiny.'

Lupita snapped.

'Why are you doing this, *all powerful* Prince?' She hadn't intended for the sarcasm to come out as strongly as it did, but ran with it anyway.

Maybe the flame of defiance still burned somewhere.

'If you are able to do this,' she said, gesturing broadly around. 'Then why seek to *bestow* anything on me at all, you have us. Cornered. You have me in...' she looked down at her attire. 'White linen wraps, apparently, but prisoner apparel nonetheless.'

She couldn't quell the anger now; it was bubbling to the surface uncontrollably.

'Why bother with this whole theatrical show?'

The Prince mused silently on her rebuttal, a hint of satisfaction evident on his face.

This is playing to your damn script still, she thundered, annoyed at herself for continuing to play to The Prince's tune.

'Because I need your compliance,' The Prince eventually said, offering his words with a fake air of vulnerability. 'I need all of your compliance. If I empower you as leader of the humans, Lupita, and you accept our offer of salvation, and myself as your ruler, I expect the other humans to follow you. I expect them to see and honour the champion that I see in you, that we all see, before us this very day.'

Words, empty words.

'It is true, I could just conquer you and demand submission,' he said, with a nonchalant flick of the hand. 'But where would that lead us? To rebellions, to death. I want your civilisation to join us as equals, and this will only happen if they follow the right leader and become accepted into the Citadel under the right *terms*.'

There was that word again, terms. Lupita had yet to hear what these terms were, but she assumed that they were not going to provide the freedom over their own lives that mankind had enjoyed up until now.

It was becoming clearer to Lupita. This whole charade. The Prince wanted one thing from her, but it wasn't to *lead*, it was to sell the illusion of choice to humanity. Let them believe that Lupita had been chosen by some higher power, so they would comply and fall into line when she *saved* them from an uncertain fate.

The memories, while humiliating and raw, were not there to break her, not really. They were there to show that she was just like everyone else, personalise her, so that the people could relate to her. So that they would endorse the *terms* that Lupita was expected to accept on behalf of all.

This was nothing short of a fraudulent election campaign on a universal scale, and Lupita was not going to let The Prince get his puppet leader.

The anger exploded out of her.

'SHOW THE REST OF IT!' she screamed high into the clouds above. 'Show them the rest of the memory!'

The Prince's image looked sharply to his left, at something not captured by the floating lights projecting his image. The pause afforded Lupita a further platform to rage.

'Show them the rest of it! Where I run out of the store crying because Jessica walked away with the coat I had spent months saving up for. Show them that I had to work two jobs, not *for the hustle* but because I needed to keep a roof over my head. Show them that I was only bilingual because my family moved here from Nigeria when I was young, and not some rich person—'

The rage within her broke.

'Extra,' she said, kicking the sand around her as she spoke. 'Curriculum.' Another kick.

'ACTIVITY!' Finally roaring.

'Show them – I don't care anymore! Show them how much I worry about wetting myself again in public following the classroom incident, so much so that sometimes I can't leave the house, how the reason my little brother was crying when we were four was because I broke his plane on *purpose*. I was an entitled little princess who didn't want to share our mother's love – let's watch that back shall we?

'Don't just show my supposed highlights reel to make me out to be this faultless and perfect leader, I am not that. I will not have the entire planet fooled into thinking I am someone I am not!'

The Prince finally reacted, snapping back to face down at Lupita, nostrils flared. It appeared he had finally lost his patience with the performance.

'You will do well to watch how you speak to me, *Child*. Your entire civilisation can be removed at a flick of my wrist, you churlish and insignificant parasite. Do you not realise that you risk the extinction of humanity just because you cannot play along?'

'But that is just it, *prince*, we are not obedient. We are flawed and we are divided. You have to cherry pick a selection of my darkest days to sell me to the masses, careful not to offend anyone. You cover up my poverty with a string of ambiguous qualities that are only acceptable or trendy when you have money, because you know the rich will never accept *a poor* leading them. You misrepresent my personality, and you literally whitewash—'

Lupita ripped at the white linen wrapped around her, grateful to see a flash of her original vest and leggings underneath.

'You hide and offset my dark skin in this pathetic white wrapping, so as not to scare the bigots and racists.'

The linen fell to the ground in ribbons at her feet.

'But through our differences,' she continued, kicking herself free of the linen. 'I think I speak for everyone, when I say that we are united against one thing, and that is against oppression. And those who wish to rule us.'

'We are not perfect, but we are, and will be, free. No human will bend the knee to you, or anyone that we haven't ourselves decided. Whether they are a king,' she concluded, hands clenched with tremendous adrenaline, 'or *just a prince*.'

The Prince writhed in fury, losing all composure.

'Then you have chosen death for your people!' he screeched, leaning down to Lupita, highlighting the imposing difference in scale between her and his hologram. 'They will all suff—'

'BUT I SPEAK TO YOU, INHABITANTS OF THIS CITADEL,' Lupita interrupted, undeterred. 'Were you not once in my shoes? Do you slave for this pathetic master wondering what your life would have been like if you didn't play his game, accept his *terms*?'

The Prince snorted, sneering down at Lupita.

'You will not *dare* to address my citizens,' he said. 'We are united agains—'

Lupita interrupted again. 'I very much doubt you are, if our own history has taught me anything it's that you cannot rule through fear without those who serve you wishing for your eventual demise.'

An idea was forming for Lupita, it wasn't complete, and she wasn't sure it would work, but it would likely buy her some time.

What was the alternative?

'Prove your rule,' Lupita posed. 'This is an amphitheatre, is it not? If I am the human champion, send someone to fight me in a fair battle. If I win, you set us free. If I lose, well, that is for you to decide.'

'You will not set the conditions for which I am to engage with you,' spat The Prince. 'This is a folly.'

'Are you scared you might lose?' INHABITANTS OF THE CITADEL.' Lupita was shouting again, mimicking the grand gestures previously exhibited by The Prince. 'WHY DO YOU FOLLOW A LEADER WHO IS AFRAID TO FIGHT?'

'I fear nothing,' dismissed The Prince. 'I can, and will, simply have you all disposed of.'

'A ruler running from a challenge, tell me, do the virtues you look for in your citizens include cowardice? It seems inherent from their leadership.' Lupita kept going. She needed him to bite, to delay whatever swift death he had planned for mankind. She was under no illusion that she could defeat anything on the Coliseum floor and doubted The Prince would honour this deal even if she did.

But that was not the purpose of this stand.

If this was to be mankind's swansong, then Lupita's last action would be with a hope to spread discord and doubt amongst the Citadel. Perhaps it can plant the seed of rebellion that will lead to freedom for some other galactic society they didn't get the chance to meet themselves.

Maybe then the existence of humanity will not have been for nothing.

Lupita did not dwell on these thoughts clearly, conscious of the open state of her mind to The Prince. However, she did use this private channel now to her advantage.

They will be watching you, all of them, not just the humans. Their eyes met, the hologram still engulfing the space above Lupita. She knew he could understand her, being fed her thoughts from some source. She kept going, mentally projecting her thoughts as articulately as possible.

Turn away from this proposal and you will appear weak to them, unfit to rule.

It seemed appropriate for it to end this way, reflected Lupita, letting a hint of sadness drip into her otherwise resolute mindset. Mankind never did move past the need for violence or fighting. If this worked, and the collective death of an entire civilisation could inspire a better one to rise up from the ashes, maybe they could achieve the peace humanity let continually evade them.

The Prince's image had disappeared at Lupita's last words, and she looked to the walls surrounding her, fearing the worst. However, moments later, his smug profile came together once more in the sky, albeit with a new suggestion of frustration. An ugly sense of cunning remained, however, sparkling behind those narrow translucent eyes.

'I accept your offer to fight for your survival,' The Prince said, carefully. 'My initial reluctance was that of surprise, this type of request is unprecedented within our traditional Trial.'

The optics of the situation must have dawned on The Prince.

It was working.

'But,' he added, holding up a finger, 'I will not sully the sacred sand beneath with bloodshed unnecessarily, not when a better option exists.'

Lupita looked up, mystified. The Prince spoke to the audience once more.

'I have released one of your number back to your planet,' he pronounced, proudly, as if excepting applause. 'Our analysis has shown that this individual personifies the warrior-like attributes needed for this situation, more so than…'

He gestured down, not finishing his sentence, letting the silent implication deafen.

'It would be unbecoming of me to not provide you with a fairer chance,' he added, smugly.

You are trying to discredit me now, thought Lupita, bitterly. *Because I showed you up.*

Before returning his gaze to the little white lights surrounding them, a satisfied glance to Lupita danced across his face.

His image dispersed, revealing what appeared to be a video feed back on earth, as if taken from a drone. As it zoomed onto the land below, The Prince's voice overlaid the image.

'I would ask you all to watch your warrior carefully, wish him success. For if he falls, you are to be dealt with as I please.'

High above in the Coliseum, beyond Lupita's vision, Jusic observed from the Sanctum's window. Slowly spinning his quarterstaff in his hand, he watched the developments, brow furrowed.

This was troubling.

Earth

Lin had been busy.

Following the near miss at the security door, he ran straight to the building's evidence room down the corridor, kicking open the frame this time in lieu of his key card.

Once inside, he rooted around for appropriate protection. His search was short, thankfully, as, not long after rummaging through the shelves of clear exhibit bags, he came across two cases of interest.

The first was a modern hatchet, used by a would-be

aggravated robber in a failed attempt for a local cash machine. The other was a partial suit of armour, submitted to the lab for blood spatter analysis following a country manor murder in Sussex.

Lin ripped all the bags open, cringing at the number of infractions and miscarriages of justice he was causing.

Jasper. He reminded himself, considering his actions justified under the circumstances.

He picked up the hatchet first and made his way over to the firearms cabinet in the corner, hastily striking the lock and grabbing an armful of the rifles and ammo inside. The drugs and narcotics locker next to him also received a similar treatment, and Lin briefly perused the contents inside in the same way he would a vending machine.

It wasn't that he was looking to get high, although a level of escapism at the moment was certainly tempting – but more a contingency. He found what he was looking for at the bottom, nestled carefully under some scales and a block of hashish. It was a syringe full of morphine, exhibited from an elderly domestic abuse case that he had examined for fingerprints earlier in the month. Opening the bag, he slid the capped plunger out and wrapped it around his leg with some exhibit tape.

If all seemed truly hopeless, he would rather go out in a peaceful, drug-induced haze, than to the jaws on the beasts he could hear wailing outside.

With the equipment sorted, Lin had quickly moved away from the labs to the offices on the first floor. He wasn't sure how long he would have internet access for, or even electricity, so he needed to act fast and print off as many emergency manuals as he could. As all six office printers whirled online and clunked into life to produce the first tranche of survival guidance, Lin finally checked his phone.

Dialling all his contacts from his ex-wife to the emergency services, even his local car garage, gave the same outcome – no answer. Desperately, he also briefly checked his regular internet haunts for signs of life on the forums, however, there was nothing to suggest anyone was out there.

What did draw his eye however, was the time.

14:37.

Lin studied the numbers, baffled. How could it only be 14:37? He had sent a message to his ex-wife at 14:03 saying that the traffic on the way to the park had been busy so he might be dropping Jasper off late. Now it was dark outside though, as if it was much later.

He walked to the edge of the office to look up at the sky through one of the large, tinted windows.

It certainly was dark, but not because it was late in the day. The sky was dominated by a large, black, spherical entity. As large as a planet, nestled neatly between earth and the moon, various complex protrusions and blinking lights could all be seen dotting its surface.

It dawned on Lin that he was possibly not looking at another planet, however, but a space station.

Brilliant, he thought, cynically.

Sarcasm aside, however, he felt a surprising sense of relief. He wasn't alone.

Lin glanced down, only now really registering the roaming beasts that littered the roads surrounding Erogen Forensics. There was a connection between these events, he was sure of it, and then also an opportunity – he just needed to survive long enough to pull the pieces together properly.

Feeling inspired, Lin noticed a small number of the beasts outside laying still on the ground, deceased.

Attrition, most likely, he surmised, looking at their bodies for further clues.

The beasts that chased Lin had tried to bite him, as if

driven by a hunger. It was not out of the question for them to need sustenance in order to survive, something the apparent absence of humanity, as well as Lin locking himself in the building, had stolen from them.

This posed a more pressing question, however.

How was Lin going to endure a siege of beasts here?

The walls seemed to hold them back for now. Evidently, they lacked the required intelligence to problem solve and break down the doors. But what of food? Lin had access to a vending machine or two within the building, but nothing that would sustain him for long.

Lin screwed up his face, considering the options available while letting the sound of the printers whirling around the room wash over him. He looked out past the moving figures in the road below to the corner of a building that lay just a few short roads away.

It was a supermarket.

Ideally, a quick visit to this supermarket to grab as much long-life food as possible would do the trick, perhaps even some extra water in case the pipes failed. He would then be able to truly bunker down until he figured out how to communicate with the space station, and hopefully find out where Jasper and everyone went.

How many 'long-life' items were likely to be in this supermarket though? Tins were cumbersome, and he didn't fancy spending time looking at expiration dates while salivating monsters nipped at his neck.

Lin left the window and walked to the closet bathroom to ponder this problem, sealing the plugs in the sinks and turning on the taps to fill the basins. Food was a requirement, but he also needed water. And while the pipes continued to work, he should collect as much as he could.

Returning his thoughts back to the supermarket, Lin recalled the huge walk-in freezers that the forensic site had to hold DNA samples. They were downstairs next to the evidence store and were large enough to store a significant amount of food potentially. This meant Lin was not limited to long-life food, but just about anything that could be frozen.

Great, so he could smash in and grab just about anything. Reducing the time he was exposed out in the open seemed sensible and certainly made the excursion more likely to succeed.

Did he need to worry about electricity? Probably at some point. The building had a back-up generator to protect it from power cuts, particularly important for keeping the DNA samples frozen in such an event. The back-up generator ran on petrol and luckily there were enough cars in the car park for Lin to be able to syphon the required amount. It wasn't without risk, and not likely to be viable in the long run, but it gave him time.

Lin quickly darted to the nearest computer and typed in the next cohort of printouts he would want.

How to syphon petrol from a car. He clicked the first Wikihow link and pressed print.

Back-up generator maintenance. This took a few scrolls to get past the adverts but he found an appropriate link. Print.

Long term drinking water treatment. Another one, print.

And lastly, *Nearest airbases and airports.*

This last one was an emerging thought, something that Lin needed to dwell on further. If he was to try and make contact with the planet-sized ship in the sky for some answers to this madness, he was likely at best to need radio communication equipment.

At worst, though, he might need to fly up there himself.

Lin made a mental note to print out instruction manuals on common planes at some point, just in case of this eventuality, however that was not the priority right now.

Printing queue organised in an apocalypse, Lin burst from the office, running back down to the evidence room to gear up. He needed to act quickly before he overthought the complexity of what he was about to do. Once he had the food in the walk-in freezers, though, he could plan his next move with a bit more headspace.

Lin weaved through the corridors, arriving at the heap of armour and torn bags on the floor of the evidence room he had left earlier. It looked cumbersome, but if the beasts were going to be biting him primarily, some protection to his fleshly limbs would go a long way.

Sliding on the armour proved immediately difficult by himself however and Lin found he could only squeeze on a single arm of armour and a chainmail vest before his movement became too restricted.

This would have to do, he could lead with his armoured left arm, drawing the beast's jaws to the steel plates adorning it whilst then also aiming and firing the rifles with his right.

Easy.

Lin bound his exposed skin with evidence tape, thickly applying it to provide additional protection but also flexibility. He wasn't sure it would stop a tooth or two, but it was the best he could do under the circumstances. He attached the hatchet to his belt and checked on the syringe of morphine taped to his leg. After loading the rifles with appropriate ammunition and fastening them to him for easy access, he stood back at the security door he had scrabbled into, facing the illuminous green emergency exit sign with apprehension.

Here we go, he narrated, as if encouraging his legs to make the first move. He picked up and donned a heavy motorbike helmet he found in the evidence bags earlier, sealing his head and neck.

Get out, find a car with the keys still in, grab provisions, get back. With a final nod to himself, Lin pressed the security door's release bar to swing the door open. He held his armoured arm out in front, using it to rest the barrel of the rifle he was aiming down, ready to fire should anything be on the other side.

The Sanctum

Jusic studied the monitor with trepidation.

The human, whom he now understood to be called 'Lin' from his computer log in, charged out of his fortification with purpose, firing lethal projectiles at a group of approaching Thræll.

Jusic found the firearms enthralling. The Citadel had always restricted weapons to the populace, Jusic himself was only one of very few even allowed anything more than a spear or dagger, his mystical quarterstaff a symbol of his rank.

Several Thræll fell instantly, leaving just one remaining in the immediate area which dodged two successive shots and dived towards Lin, mouth wide. Lin dragged his steel arm in the air, jamming it between the open jaws of the Thræll. With his other hand, Lin dropped the rifle and picked up the hatchet to his side, swinging his free arm round and embedding the blade deep into the caught Thræll's neck.

Incredible, noted Jusic as he watched the now lifeless Thræll slide off Lin's arm with a limp thud.

Perhaps The Sisters were not needed after all.

The reminder of The Sisters' presence on earth unsettled Jusic however. With the feed of Lin's last stand being played to the whole Citadel as part of the Trial, the risk of them being spotted while culling the Thræll was high. He could only hope that they were being discreet.

The terminal hummed before Jusic, its screens drowning him in a glut of artificial light. He glanced at the image of Lupita on the monitor to his left, standing unbroken on the dusty Coliseum floor. She had shown incredible resilience to The Prince's manipulations, more so than any Trial he had seen before.

He couldn't help feel a rising spiritual connection with the antagonistic creature that stood before his liege.

Lin's monitor caught his attention and Jusic watched the human dive into an abandoned vehicle just as a swarm of Thræll descended. The vehicle kicked into gear immediately, skidding violently before lurching forward down the road. The Thræll could not comprehend the danger and stayed charging, seconds later being mowed down by Lin.

Jusic wondered what the atmosphere was like in the Royal Palace currently with The Prince's gambit going the way that it was. He did not envy his fellow inquisitors by his side.

A thought was nagging him. Lin the human was calling out a name when he first awoke from the botched Collection. Jasper.

Jusic activated his third monitor and searched the Collection archive, finding a young Jasper under room C#82872. The feed opened up revealing a moderately sized room, the typical type of confinement, with thanks to Tetradonite shrinking technology, that existed in each individual tiny light surrounding the Coliseum.

Jasper could be seen sitting on one of the beds supplied to each room, watching the footage of his father hurtling down the road. He was just a small human, no older than five star cycles at most. He was clapping though, cheering his father on as he careened around the abandoned vehicles towards a large structure ahead. Completely unaware of what Lin was facing down.

This bothered Jusic, who clipped the intercom in front of him.

'This is Inquisitor I'Lyr, I request C#82872 is afforded as much support and care as possible, his bloodline is one of importance to the humans. Make sure wherever he is located is of a certain privilege.'

A barbed, crackling, voice returned, 'C#82872 is not on our list of favoured individuals, Inquisitor I'Lyr, can you confirm you are asking for this child's status to be changed under your authorisation?'

I would be very much surprised if any human was on such a list currently.

'I can.'

'Very well, the preparations will be made.'

It wasn't enough. When Lin fell the humans would be enslaved, likely to the Undercity considering Lupita's insubordination. At least Jasper would likely lead a better life than he would have otherwise now. Perhaps as a farmhand rather than a servant. Try as he might, Jusic couldn't find solace in this comfort, however.

After all, it had been him who sent the Thræll after his father.

Looking back to Lin's monitor, Jusic watched as his vehicle approached a new fortification at high speed, crashing through the weak glass front doors and coming to an abrupt stop amongst now crushed shelves of produce and boxes. Lin fired at the pursing Thræll before slamming his shoulder against the vehicle door to exit.

He immediately started throwing the packages around him into his vehicle indiscriminately, firing off shots at the Thrælls that got too close. Many were starting to swarm to Lin now, the sound of the crash likely alerting their attention.

Jusic watched on, disheartened, as he saw Lin pulling the

trigger of his last rifle to no effect, ammunition depleted. He drew his hatchet and charged at the nearest Thræll, repeating his earlier steel-arm-in-the-mouth method. Despite felling the first few that approached with increasing brutality, Jusic could see more arriving to overrun the fortification.

He was helpless, Jusic convinced himself, watching Lin throw himself in the vehicle in a last-ditch attempt to avoid the horde. What could he do? Any intervention would result in the same outcome, the humans would be enslaved regardless. He could recall the Thræll, but The Prince would simply claim victory in his agreement with Lupita, likely imprisoning Jusic in the process.

Surprisingly, the Oracle's words all those years ago reverberated in his head, echoing ominously.

It seems likely that your actions could result in the Fall of the Citadel itself.

No. He would not intervene. This would not be his prophecy.

The noticeable lack of clapping from Jasper's screen to his right made him turn. The boy was now looking scared.

Jusic made a decision. While he wouldn't interfere with the outcome, the least he could do was save Jasper from witnessing the traumatic death of his father.

Thræll had ripped the doors of Lin's vehicle open, one grabbing his exposed legs and pulling the flailing human out into the open.

Jusic hit a series of buttons in front of him, typing in his authorisation with urgency.

Lin's feed disconnected with a soft click.

The Prince did not waste any time in appearing before Jusic.

'What is going on, I'Lyr? The feed has stopped.'

'I am investigating, your Highness,' lied Jusic, tapping a few buttons to the side of him to appear busy. He knew full well that The Prince would not waste the Seer's energy on reading his mind right now. 'It would appear the issue with the Collection and then this sudden loss of transmission may be linked.'

'Sabotage?'

'Quite possibly,' Jusic said convincingly, appearing both concerned and thoughtful. 'Leave it with me, your Highness, should the transmission not be recoverable is there anything you need me to prepare?'

The Prince cursed loudly, smouldering through the screen.

'No. Nothing,' he concluded curtly, leaving without another word.

The Sanctum returned to silence around Jusic, who stood at the terminal letting out a weighty sigh.

The Coliseum

The confusing pause in footage was broken with The Prince's image once again returning into view above Lupita.

'I have graciously saved you from the burden of seeing the gorier moments that followed this transmission,' he pronounced, solemnly. 'Your planetside champion fought fearlessly.'

'More tricks and deception, Prince?' asked Lupita, attempting to hide the desperation in her voice herself. 'First you cower from my challenge and then you suspiciously drop the footage. It's not a good look for you really I must admit, I wonder how many of your citizens are looking at all this with justified scepticism—'

'It is over!' bit The Prince, enraged. 'You have lost!'

'Then fight me yourself! Prove it in front of all mankind and the Citadel that you are not just a toothless oppressor.'

'Bah! What do you hope to achieve where your other champion clearly did not? I did you humans a favour by providing you with an *adequate* and *able* champion in your place.'

It was Lupita's turn to seethe.

'Face me then, you repugnant piece of shit!'

'You are nothing but a parasite to me, to face you in combat myself would grant you an honour you fall significantly short of deserving.'

'Then I hope the Citadel see you for who you really are, unsuitable to rule,' Lupita said, coldly.

'You dare—' snarled The Prince, clearly standing now from the movement in his image from above. 'Fine,' he conceded, erratically. 'You want a warrior's death, Lupita? You can have it. Guards? Descend to the Coliseum floor, show the humans how we deal with impertinence in the Citadel.'

After a short delay, four elegantly robed guards strode onto the beige sands of the Coliseum, each armed with metal tipped staves.

Lupita braced, easing back to think.

'You may not have chosen a similar path,' she said quietly to the walls surrounding her, hoping they could hear. 'But I will fight for the freedom we deserve. Submitting to The Prince's rule would have meant subjugation.'

Lupita charged.

She knew she couldn't take them, not without being armed, but pressed forward nonetheless. She needed a plan. What did she get taught in school? Prehistoric humans thrived due to their stamina and ability to continually chase their prey, long after they had worn tired.

Perhaps she could use that.

Lupita veered left from the guards, running back parallel to the Coliseum perimeter. She checked behind her to see if they were in pursuit.

They were.

She didn't need to sprint, just maintain enough pace to keep them close on her tail. Lupita was athletic enough to do this for a short time, but a further plan would be needed.

She had almost run the boundary when the guards finally pulled short, regrouping to try a different line of attack. They split into two groups without discussion. Two guards headed back on themselves while the remaining two pushed on, a pincer move to entrap Lupita.

Perfect.

She took the opportunity and doubled back, running at speed to reach the two guards while they remained split from the others.

When she was in reach, the first guard jabbed his sharpened stave towards her head, however, Lupita jerked to the right and avoided the blow. Still running, she slid under the next guard's swipe and got as close to them as possible. Long sticks would be useless in close quarters combat.

The blowy, ornate robes of the guards gave something for Lupita to grab for and she pulled herself between the guards whilst restricting their movement, bunching up the loose fabric with her fists.

As the guards looked down to see what confined them, Lupita threw up a hidden stash of sand she had picked up in her slide into the eyes of both guards.

They recoiled, blinded. Leaving an opening for Lupita to quickly kick the first guard in the chest, winding him and forcing him to drop his stave. She looked up to see the second group of guards close by now. Knowing she would be overwhelmed against all four at once, Lupita grabbed the fallen stave and backed away to the perimeter again. It was still four against one, but at least she had a weapon now.

'A courageous endeavour,' The Prince said lazily from above. 'But it will not change the outcome.'

Picking up their fourth, the guards set their remaining staves towards Lupita's direction and slowly approached. With her back to the Coliseum's edge, she found herself soon surrounded as they inched closer and closer, the sharpened weapons keeping her from running again.

Lupita threw her own down to the ground, raising her hands in submission.

'Are you happy here?' she asked the guards quietly, catching them by surprise.

They hesitated.

Lupita turned to the guard she had kicked. 'I am assuming that you will be punished by The Prince for losing your weapon?'

He didn't say anything.

'Take it back,' she said, gently kicking it back to him, letting it roll along the sand to his feet.

The voice of The Prince boomed once more around them.

'What are you planning, insolent child? You can't possibly expect mercy after your actions today.'

Lupita ignored him, holding eye contact with the guards surrounding her.

'This is your chance,' she whispered, aware that The Prince would likely hear her anyway. 'You must see what he is, a tyrant. A megalomaniac. Throw down your staves and fight with me. Let's bring change to the Citadel together.'

The Prince laughed manically above, but Lupita kept on.

'How many times has he done this? Conquered and enslaved a population. Did he do it to your people too? Are you happy as a result? How many civilisations must fall to his ego? I'm not saying that if you join me that we will win, we will be few against many, but we might set a precedent, send a message, that freedom will always be worth fighting for. That oppression should never be accepted.'

The guards remained still, unwavering, as their weapons stayed raised towards her. Lupita's last gambit had failed, and she slumped her shoulders in defeat, leaning back against the stonework pillar behind her and sliding down to the granular sand beneath.

It was over. She could not spark a flame of rebellion, the intended enduring gift of humanity, it had all been for nothing.

What Lupita did not realise though, was that high above her in the Sanctum, stood the fuse she was looking for.

Jusic watched down to the Coliseum floor, dismayed. He wasn't sure what he was more horrified about, the fact he was about to witness bloodshed on the sacred sands for the first time in his career or the fact that Lupita's speech was awakening something in him.

The Oracle's words still lapped against his consciousness, like a gentle tide against the shore.

Was this the moment?

The edges of the Coliseum below twinkled with activity and Jusic noticed a further stream of The Prince's personal guards entering the arena. He was using this opportunity as a show of strength.

Lupita remained backed to the wall, defeated. She was no longer convincing the guards to lay down their arms, just sitting there, beaten.

The guards awaited The Prince's final call to land the finishing blow.

It did not matter if this was the moment the Oracle had prophesied anymore, Jusic decided.

He would not be silent.

He snatched at his quarterstaff, rapping it on top of the Tetradonite bench to his side causing it to instantly diminish. After picking up the now small cuboid, Jusic strode to the back of the room, turning to face the large pane of glass separating the Sanctum from the Coliseum.

He took a moment to exhale, resigning himself, before throwing the cuboid in the air in front of him, twirling his quarterstaff and swinging it like a bat in one smooth move. He struck the object hard, firing it towards the window as it rapidly grew back to the size of a bench. The momentum of the hit remained despite the object's change in size, resulting in the bench colliding with the glass with such velocity that it shattered it entirely, sailing through and allowing Jusic the entrance he needed to get to Lupita in time.

He dashed forward, leaping through the opening with a sharp bound. As he sailed past the jagged edges of the broken window, he twisted in the air, pivoting to face the Sanctum and the wall of trinkets at the back. He aimed the tip of his staff at the Khappit Scimitar, snapping back his arm in a sharp pull causing the weapon to wrench from his mantel towards him.

Jusic caught it with an outreached hand as he started to plummet down the Coliseum's spire, robes fluttering in his wake. He did the same sharp jolt with his staff to the large bench falling in front of him, returning it to normal size and his hand in mid-air.

He was now plunging past the millions of white lights surrounding the Coliseum walls towards the beige desert ground below. Lupita was in sight, still surrounded on all sides but looking up at the commotion his spectacular entrance undoubtedly caused.

Slowing himself with a pulse of his staff, Jusic hit the ground hard and rolled to absorb the impact as much as he could, taking out the legs of a few bewildered guards near him with a swipe of his weapon. He bounced to his feet instantly, twisting the quarterstaff in the air to crack it on the helmets of the guards remaining upright around him.

They sprawled to the ground, unconscious, as residual clusters of glass from the Sanctum's breakout above showered them gently.

Jusic turned to Lupita as she stood to her feet, unsure what his intentions were. He then brandished the ornate scimitar he had pulled from the Sanctum from under his robes, causing Lupita to flinch.

Jusic smiled, handing her the blade handle first.

'Fear not,' he said calmly. 'We may not survive this.'

Lupita accepted the weapon, warily.

'But I will fight for your right to freedom regardless, as long as you will have me.'

She looked to the guards at his feet, and then to those cautiously approaching them behind him. She finally looked to Jusic, nodding gently before stepping forward beside him. She raised her weapon across her face, steadying her stance to charge forward.

'Thank you,' Lupita said with a side glance to Jusic.

'No, I can assure you, the gratitude is all mine.'

A sense of release washed over Jusic. A weight he hadn't noticed bearing him down was suddenly evaporating from his shoulders. Lupita had provided him the right amount of encouragement to finally reject his entrapment, and as he stood in the Coliseum, essentially a traitor to his people, he finally felt the hallmarks of a purpose long ignored.

Still the guards approached, unrelenting.

The Prince's voice was the first sound to break the deadlock. It came from above, as thunderous as before, but only now did it show any real spontaneity, the standard script now abandoned.

'Inquisitor I'Lyr,' he said, hiding the rage and surprise in his voice poorly. 'It is a privilege for you to join us.'

'I stand here, your Highness,' Jusic returned, looking up

to the looming bust of The Prince as he spoke. 'For all the times that I stood by and did nothing.'

'Nothing? Jusic? You were instrumental to many of our Trials, or did you forget your input in your rashness to play hero?'

'I do not deny my previous involvement in this sham,' Jusic admitted, bitterly. 'But as I believe the humans themselves say, the best time to plant a tree is 20 years ago, the second best time is now. And so here I am, now, finally doing what I should have done for all those civilisations we lost along the way.'

'Then you will die a fool, Inquisitor.'

'But a content one, *Nazeem*.'

The use of The Prince's real name sent a rapid hush around the Coliseum floor. Many watching the exchange would likely be surprised to hear it, only knowing him as The Prince for all their lives. Despite the attempt to outlaw its use, it survived generations through whispered word of mouth in most cases. For Jusic, though, he was there when The Prince was known just as Inquisitor Nazeem.

'Kill the scum!' barked The Prince. 'Focus on the Inquisitor, I want to stand over his dying corpse first.'

He ended his transmission, the holographic lights in the sky dimming and returning the daunting scale of the Coliseum's tower to the combatants on the ground.

Jusic steadied himself, twirling his staff lazily around his hand, thinking. A low hum was distracting him, however.

What was that?

The noise was getting louder, while still muffled and nondescript, it appeared to swallow them all on the sacred sands. Jusic looked to the Coliseum walls, it was coming from The Collected.

'They stand with you,' Jusic said to Lupita, motioning to the white lights with a nod of his head. He had not heard

The Collected make enough noise together before. It was rhythmic, like a chant almost. Just the fact they could make any sound from the confines of their tiny rooms was impressive.

'What will happen to them?' Lupita shouted over the growing noise.

'He won't waste the numbers seen here, they are too useful to the Citadel,' returned Jusic. 'Many will be enslaved. Unless of course, we can stop—'

He wasn't able to finish his sentence as the nearest guard made the first attack, darting forward in a hope to take him by surprise. Jusic sidestepped while hooking his own staff behind the aggressors leading leg, pivoting to slam his body weight into the guard to send him toppling.

'Roarq,' he said, recognising the guard. 'You don't have to do this. Fight alongside us.'

'You know I can't.' The man known as Roarq struggled as he lay on the floor, looking panicked. 'I have a family.'

Jusic raised his staff above Roarq as if to strike, looking to the other approaching guards for movement.

'Then you know what I'm about to do comes from self-preservation and nothing more, I'm sorry,' Jusic said, sympathetically.

'Do it, please,' begged Roarq, before turning to a whisper, or what constituted as close to a whisper against the commotion of the human war cries around them. 'Some of them will fight for you, if you start to win, but only a few. Others are loyal to the Palace.'

'Play dead then, join us when you are ready,' Jusic whispered back.

Lupita stepped forward, standing close to the two of them.

'How do we know who is loyal and who isn't?' she asked.

'Khappit rings,' Roarq replied, eyeing Jusic and the staff

he held above his head. 'Worn on the index finger of those sympathetic to the resistance movement.'

More and more guards shifted forward now. Another took Roarq's lead and made a move for Lupita. She parried the stave with a flick of her scimitar, surprised by her own competence with the blade.

A third guard now stepped forward, allowing the second to recoil from Lupita's blow. He jabbed his weapon towards her head, the metal tip pausing just short of her face. Perplexed, he went to push it forward again as Lupita snapped her head back, nodding in thanks to Jusic beyond the guard. He turned around to see Jusic pointing his quarterstaff at the stave's metal tip, freezing it in the air. The guard let go of the now floating stick and turned to charge at Jusic, who lurched his quarterstaff back behind him, causing the motionless stave to leap towards them both, striking the guard down from behind.

'We won't be able to turn the tide,' admitted Lupita breathlessly, slicing through a subsequent guard's horizontal stave before thrusting a foot into his chest to knock him back. 'Do you have a plan?'

'No,' Jusic replied, dancing past Lupita swinging wildly. He connected both ends of his quarterstaff with two aggressors, juddering the weapon back and forth between their heads until they fell. A loud war cry above screeched, wrenching Jusic's attention up to glance at the upper Coliseum. The Prince's bust was still absent. Squinting, he picked out movement high up on the arena's walls. 'No, but they might.'

Down descended The Sisters, sliding from the Sanctum's broken window. Ashren and Tiki were ahead, daggers grinding the wall as they slowed their fall. Vhe was just behind, an unidentifiable mass slung over her shoulder.

Jusic motioned to Lupita to head towards their landing

and the two of them ducked, weaved and brawled until they made it to the Coliseum's far edge.

Ashren was the first to touch down, leaping from the wall above them to land on two charging guards, daggers sinking into both. Tiki followed, spinning in the air to release a wave of shurikens. Some connecting and dropping the guards nearest. Most, however, pierced the sand around Lupita and Jusic, acting as a line that Tiki dared the guards to cross.

'I can't ask you to die for me,' Jusic said as the sand settled from their arrival. 'Go, run from here. Or you will be branded my accomplice.'

'We did not swear an oath to House I'Lyr for a long life,' replied Ashren, ripping her daggers from the guards beneath her. 'We swore for a fun one,' she said, winking.

'I release you of your oath, please, you must escape.'

'Oh you release the oath?' Tiki asked, feigning interest. 'Well that changes everything.'

Ashren smiled at Jusic warmly, despite the urgent frustration on his face.

'If this fight is important enough for you to die for, then that's reason enough for us to fight by your side.' She walked up to Jusic and embraced him fiercely. Tiki nodded in solidarity behind her.

'Besides,' Ashren added, releasing a stunned Jusic, and turning to face Lupita. 'Vhe in particular has grown quite fond of these ones.'

As if on cue, Vhe dropped down beside them, rolling what appeared to be a half suit of armour off her shoulder.

'These meatbags are quite resourceful actually, Jusic,' Vhe proclaimed with an uncharacteristic sense of admiration. She pulled what was now evidently a human up from the floor to stand.

Lin held a complicated expression. He nodded quickly in

gratitude to Vhe, trying his best to not look utterly lost. The Sisters had explained some of the context to him after their rescue at the supermarket, but despite their best efforts, Lin found himself not entirely sure where he was now, or what he was supposed to be doing.

He thought back to when he was printing off agriculture and survival guides off the internet.

Simpler times, he reminisced, taking in the enormity of the guard infested arena they now stood in.

A wave of activity around them surged into focus and guards began to charge past Tiki's warning markers to the small group that lay beyond. Lupita was the first to move, she weaved past where The Sisters and Jusic stood to kneel at the ground where Lin had been placed by Vhe. She picked up a discarded hatchet and handed it to her fellow human.

'Care to go out swinging?' she asked, smirking, as Lin snatched at the handle eagerly.

'Are these still bitey bitey ones?' he asked, watching the guards move toward.

'Less bitey bitey, more stabby stabby,' replied Lupita, readying herself.

'Oh good, nice to have a change at least.'

Lin paused, feeling the weight of the axe in his hands while taking in the growing roars of the trapped humans surrounding them. 'Can they hear us?' he asked eventually.

'Apparently.' Lupita looked up, trying her best to ignore the magnitude of the situation.

'JASPER!' Lin yelled into the noise, catching Lupita by surprise. 'DON'T WORRY, IT'S ALL GOING TO BE OKAY.' He glanced across to Tiki who had jumped into the fray of guards ahead of him, daggers whirling. The lie felt bitter on his tongue. 'Please close your eyes, Jasper,' Lin begged softly, hoping his son wouldn't see what was about to come.

'He is to be looked after, Lin the Thrællslayer.' Jusic had stepped forward beside Lin, addressing him for the first time since their arrival. Before continuing, he motioned to Ashren to watch out for a flurry of attacks behind her while swinging his own staff to fend off an attack to his right. 'Arrangements have been made to protect him.'

Lin turned to face Jusic, sizing up the impressively robed being beside him with an air of suspicion. Jusic understood the apprehension, expected it in fact, but he didn't have time to reassure the human of his allegiance right now.

A stave whistled towards them, thrown meekly by a far guard. Lin caught the spearhead in the crook of his armour-plated arm, stopping the projectile from piercing Jusic's leg. He swung his hatchet down on the middle of the stave, snapping it in two before picking up the now shorter spear to throw back into the advancing crowd.

Vhe now danced to the front of the vanguard next to Jusic, running a blade along the torsos of the guards who had been too slow to see her. She sidestepped a lunge from a stave and placed her back to Jusic's.

He understood the intention and held his back to hers in return, rotating them both slowly as they fended off the guards at all angles.

'Why did you save him?' Jusic said, casually launching a guard back to the other end of the Coliseum with a well-timed pulse.

Vhe had expected the question, just perhaps after the battle.

'He fought valiantly, Jusic, more so than most would have against those odds. We couldn't just leave him to the Thræll. I thought you would want to meet him.' She was not accustomed to blushing, and so hid it poorly despite having her back to him.

'You did the right thing, Vhe, and while I'm eternally

grateful that you are here, you must know that part of me wishes you were not.'

Vhe grinned, pivoting around to face him.

'Don't get soft on me now, Jusic.'

She lifted her daggers, both held backwards defensively. 'Just because I'm willing to die to defend them doesn't make them any less meat—'

The metal tip of a thrown stave erupted through Vhe's throat.

Vhe fell forward into Jusic's arms, confusion and agony flashing across her face before it was buried in his embrace.

Jusic snapped his attention to the centre of the Coliseum, scanning for the source of the launched stave. With a crippling sense of dread showering him, he found what he was looking for.

The Prince stood tall facing them, striding confidently towards where the defenders fought at the edge of the arena. Crown and royal embellishments aside, he was easy to pick out against the sea of beige and white robes. The Prince wore an immaculate gold and dark purple gown that billowed loftily behind as he walked. In his left hand he carried his own quarterstaff, a sinister root-shaped staff that curled and knotted asymmetrically. In his other, he yanked on a chain, dragging in his wake the Avian Seer who had been reading Lupita's mind.

The chants of the humans grew to terrifying levels, spurred on by Vhe's collapse. White lights started to flicker above, undoubtedly some the captives were trying to break free of their confinement. The chants were becoming clearer as more and more joined in the same rhythmic chorus.

LU-PI-TA

LU-PI-TA

Jusic carefully laid Vhe on the floor to her side, not wanting to move the stave from her neck. Her now vacant stare confirmed what he had feared. He barely heard Tiki screech to his side, a mournful cry at the loss of her Sister.

Jusic turned to her quickly, searching for her in the melee.

'Don't let it be in vain,' he commanded, snatching at his quarterstaff with an invigorated rage. 'Focus on The Prince.'

Tiki bared her teeth and pivoted to face Vhe's killer, dashing forwards. Jusic sent a pulse from his staff to launch her into the air above the guards ahead.

The Prince raised his own staff, freezing Tiki airborne in front of him.

'Do you consider me a fool, I'Lyr?' he asked rhetorically, cocking his head to observe the Serpentine he held captive.

'I knew allowing these redundant creatures to serve you was a mistake, how *dare* they interfere and rescue that pathetic human from the planet.'

'They did so on my orders; I threatened them to do as I commanded against their own judgement,' tried Jusic, shouting.

'He lies, Sire,' clicked the Avian to The Prince's side, hobbling forward to tug at his purple robes. 'He is trying to protect the Serpentines.'

The Prince grinned manically.

'I do not need a Seer to see through Inquisitor I'Lyr's pathetic attempts to protect his guards.'

A sudden tug to his side caught The Prince's attention. Ashren had made her way forward into the breach where he stood, slipping behind the Seer to wrap her arm around his neck and stabbing him in the back.

The Prince roared as the Avian fell, yanking the chain towards him to send the lifeless seer and Ashren into his reach.

He caught her by the neck.

Still the white lights above them flickered, the sound of the humans grew.

'YOU WILL CEASE THIS MADNESS!' he screamed

above the chaos, turning to face Jusic, both Tiki and Ashren within his control. 'CAN YOU NOT SEE YOU HAVE LOST?'

Jusic didn't dignify The Prince with a response, he spun his staff to knock back the guards now to his side and pointed it at Tiki, sending a powerful pulse to knock her from the hold The Prince's staff had her in.

He then swiftly jabbed an approaching guard in the face, causing him to release his stave. Jusic caught it before it hit the ground, swivelling to launch it like a javelin right at Ashren who remained in The Prince's grasp.

Ashren ripped a hand off The Prince's grip to catch the stave before it hit her, drawing the weapon down in an arc on his arm.

The Prince howled, releasing Ashren. Before she could react, however, the incensed Prince raised his quarterstaff above his head and slammed it into the ground between his feet, sending a powerful shockwave out and knocking Ashren and the guards within his immediate vicinity flying.

Jusic held his stance against the quake and went to charge. The Prince however had recovered quickly, pointing his weapon to Lin and Lupita who had been defending each other at the boundary of the Coliseum.

Both lurched unexpectedly towards The Prince, pulled by an invisible force. Jusic pointed his own staff at the humans, trying to break The Prince's hold.

It was futile, however, The Prince was far stronger. And, try as he might, Jusic could only slow Lin and Lupita's approach. They slowly dragged towards The Prince, trying to fight themselves free. Jusic held onto his staff, shaking with the struggle to combat The Prince's power. Several guards reached him, pulling at his weapon. He kept it aimed at the humans, even as more guards jumped up to disarm him, beating him with their staves.

'Was it worth it?' smirked The Prince as he pulsed Lupita's scimitar to the other side of the Coliseum, disarming her. Next was Lin's hatchet, which he released from his clenched fist to sink into the sand beneath them.

They were now in front of The Prince, close enough to see the feverish hunger in his eyes. He forced them to kneel in front of him, laughing triumphantly.

'It was always going to end like this.'

The white lights flashed violently around them, several turning red, the chants of humanity reaching uncontrollable levels. The rhythm remained.

LU-PI-TA

LU-PI-TA

She looked up to The Prince, finally glad to be staring into the whites of his eyes rather than a distant hologram.

'We will never serve you,' Lupita muttered.

'No you won't, because you will be dead, but they will,' he said, casually.

'Not if we kill you first.' Lin shrugged.

The Prince turned to him, using his staff to raise Lin to meet him eye to eye, dangling his body a few feet above the ground.

'You dare threaten me?' The Prince whispered, sneering.

Lin just smiled, jutting out his leg suddenly to Lupita who remained kneeling on the sand just below him.

Without needing to look, Lupita snatched at the syringe still taped to Lin's leg, leaping from the ground to sink the plunger through The Prince's thin purple robes and emptying the morphine into his body.

The Prince staggered back, aghast, dropping Lin from his control. He tried to swing his staff towards Lupita, but his strength began to fail him, falling to one knee as he laboured for breath.

An eruption of bodies behind them sent guards flying,

Jusic stood with his quarterstaff impaled in the ground between his feet. The shockwave from Jusic's blast knocked The Prince onto his back.

Beyond his sprawled, gasping body rose the figures of Tiki and Ashren. Leaping through the air, Ashren held the Khappit Scimitar high above her as she soared forward towards The Prince. She landed just shy of his body, swinging the scimitar down to sever The Prince's staff-holding arm from his body.

The Prince couldn't cry out, despite his eyes screaming with unbridled wrath. Tiki landed next to him, sinking her daggers into The Prince's chest, twisting them violently.

The Prince shook, his lips trying to formulate one last taunt. His eyes darted from Lin to Lupita, from Ashren to Tiki and then finally resting on Jusic, as the Inquisitor strode forward towards them.

'It was always going to end like this,' echoed Jusic, solemnly, watching as the life drained from his former liege. Dark blood seeped into the sands where The Prince's arm lay detached, the soft green glow of his quarterstaff dissipating.

Lupita, Lin, Ashren, Tiki and Jusic stood around the fallen Prince, unsure of what this meant. The chants of humanity had shifted, they were now cheers of jubilation, hysterical and raw. Jusic was the first to speak of the group.

'We don't have time to dither.' He was acutely aware of how much space they were being given by the guards suddenly, instead, they appeared to be more focused on attacking each other now, or running.

Jusic looked to the Coliseum walls, many of the white lights continued to flicker in the commotion, a significant amount now red.

'The Citadel is on the brink of collapse; it appears our actions may have triggered a long brewing rebellion.'

'How do we get mankind back to earth?' asked Lupita, wrenching the scimitar from the floor to wield it once more.

Jusic turned to the human, eyeing the weapon in thought.

'Returning The Collected to the planet is straightforward, what isn't, however, are the ones who have escaped into the Citadel itself.' He again glanced up. 'Several thousand will be loose by the looks of the red lights, we need to contain them quickly. Many of the Citadel's population will likely be mistaken as loyalists to The Prince and I fear misplaced retribution to the innocent that inhabit here. I will accompany you and Lin as humanity's champions to shepherd those lost. They should listen to you.'

Lupita was holding the scimitar to her side, Jusic used the tip of his quarterstaff to raise it up as he spoke.

'Carry this with you, if the hidden rebellion is using Khappit rings to distinguish themselves, those of the Citadel sympathetic to the rebellion will likely trust someone carrying the blade, even if they are human. We will not have the time to identify friend or foe any other way.'

Lin stepped forward, unstrapping his armoured arm.

'I'm afraid, *Inquisitor*, I have no interest in protecting your inhabitants. I need to find my son.'

Jusic exhaled carefully, thinking.

'An understandable priority,' he conceded. 'But much is at stake. I assure you; Jasper is safe until we can contain this transition of power.'

Lin shook his head. Holding a challenging stare to Jusic.

'Your assurances mean nothing to me, I assure you the similarities between your robes and those of the men who tried to kill us has not gone unnoticed.'

Ashren stiffened.

'Take care how you talk to the Inquisitor, human.'

Jusic hovered an impatient hand.

'Thank you, Ashren, but the Thrællslayer can be forgiven for his scepticism, he is not wrong to doubt me. Tiki?'

The Sister lifted her head.

'Take The Prince's staff and escort Lin to C#82872 to recover his son, protect them and get them home. Lupita and I will return the Thræll and reverse The Collection. Once done, we will rally the escaped humans and hope to bring some order. Lin, your species will likely be in turmoil upon returning and will seek answers and guidance. They all watched you survive the horrors of the Trial today, prepare yourself to be thrusted into a position to lead.'

Tiki bowed, picking up the mangled staff, and turned towards an arena exit. Lin lingered to hold Jusic's gaze a moment longer, before nodding lightly to follow.

'And what of me?' Ashren asked.

Jusic hesitated, looking beyond Ashren to the body of Vhe that lay askew.

'Give Vhe the burial she deserves.'

They both fell quiet for a pause before Jusic continued. 'I'm not sure what will happen to the Citadel following...'

He gestured broadly to The Prince's lifeless body.

'...whatever this is now. But getting Vhe out of here is important. Take her down to the planet and bury her somewhere appropriate.'

Ashren bowed, before somewhat reluctantly turning to approach Vhe's body. She picked her up with care, removing the stave and carried her towards an arena exit.

Lupita watched her go.

'I'm sorry for your loss,' she said heavily.

'As am I.' Jusic resisted saying more, he wasn't in the right environment to grieve.

Lupita looked to the dispersing crowd, some running some chasing. Many remained on the sands of the Coliseum, unmoving. Several by her hand.

'We would have all died or been enslaved if it wasn't for your intervention,' she admitted, not knowing exactly what to say to Jusic.

He contemplated his response, looking to the scene around them himself.

'Indeed,' he said finally, 'and now I ask you for support myself, to save my people. I know you must want nothing more than to go home, but the Citadel will fall if we don't stabilise what we have done today.'

Lupita smiled softly, respectfully mimicking the bow The Sisters gave him.

'Lead the way, Inquisitor.'

Jusic returned the smile, wavering his hand.

'We are hardly in the environment where such pageantry would be expected. Please call me Jusic.'

Lupita rose from the bow.

'What way?' she asked, looking to the exits surrounding them.

'Up.'

Jusic placed his pocketed cuboid on the ground, so it stood vertically, and pressed his quarterstaff against it gently. The object expanded rapidly as he held the two together and he stepped up, offering Lupita his hand, as the platform grew past them. He left his staff in contact as the cuboid grew into a pillar, higher and higher into the vacant air of the Coliseum.

Jusic slowed the growth as they neared the Sanctum's broken window high above the arena floor. Lupita dared a look over the side to the increasingly distant floor below.

'You jumped from here?!' she exclaimed, incredulous.

'I liked the speech you gave and thought it deserved a really dramatic entrance,' he said with a wink, releasing his quarterstaff from the pillar to allow them both to step comfortably over the broken glass and into the gentle red light of The Sanctum.

THE ANNALS OF AMAR PLAYLIST

Make One Man Weep, Another Woman Sing
- Power of Love – Huey Lewis and the News
- What is love – Haddaway
- This Year's Love – David Gray
- Love Will Tear Us Apart – Joy Division
- Wicked Game – Chris Isaac
- I Would Do Anything for Love – Meatloaf
- Silver Springs – Fleetwood Mac
- The Scientist – Coldplay
- Black – Pearl Jam

Those Hurt in the Doorway of Change Will Be Those Who Stood Still
- The Times They Are A-Changin' – Bob Dylan
- Change – Blind Melon
- Edge of Seventeen – Stevie Nicks
- Man in the Mirror – Michael Jackson
- Winds of Change – Scorpions
- I Just Want To Sell Out My Funeral – The Wonder Years
- Imagine – John Lennon

Heretic's Descent Hidden Track
- 1612 – Vulfpeck

Jusic, Hasira, David and others will all return in…

THE DESERT
OF THE REAL

VOLUME II

CPSIA information can be obtained
at www.ICGtesting.com
Printed in the USA
BVHW011529300123
657433BV00026B/960

9 781915 229878